Riggs' Ruin

Kings Reapers MC

Nicola Jane

Copyright ©2020 by Nicola Jane

All rights reserved.

No portion of this book may be reproduced in any form without written permission from the publisher or author, except as permitted by U.K. copyright law.

Meet the Team

Cover Designer: Charli Childs, Cosmic Letterz Design
Editor: Rebecca Vazquez
Proofreader: Amanda Tabor
Formatter: Nicola Miller
Publisher: Nicola Jane

Disclaimer:

This book is a work of fiction. The names, characters, places, and incidents are all products of the author's imagination and are not to be construed as real. Any similarities are entirely coincidental.

Acknowledgments

To my faithful readers, you are the reason I am still here writing. Your kind words and support are forever appreciated. Thanks for loving my stories as much as I do. xx

Paul, the reason I am still sain. You believed in me and encouraged me and here we are today, hopefully, about to provide a good life for our two boys. I love you. xx

Rebecca and Jackie, I love being a part of the mean girls, you're the best, and I couldn't do this without you. xx

Trigger Warning

Although this is an MC romance, remember, it's an MC romance.

If you're expecting hearts and flowers, you purchased the wrong book. These guys are rough, tough and sometimes out of my control.

Their story will not please everyone, but it's the story from my head, using my characters. I won't be offended if you don't like it, but I will, if you choose to ignore this warning and then cry about it.

Happy reading :) xx

Contents

Playlist	IX
Chapter 1	1
Chapter 2	11
Chapter 3	20
Chapter 4	28
Chapter 5	39
Chapter 6	51
Chapter 7	62
Chapter 8	71
Chapter 9	81
Chapter 10	93
Chapter 11	103
Chapter 12	112
Chapter 13	122
Chapter 14	132
Chapter 15	144
Chapter 16	156
Chapter 17	167
Chapter 18	175

Chapter 19	186
Chapter 20	198
Chapter 21	202
A note from me to you	208

Playlist

Take Your Time - Sam Hunt
Sorry - Halsey
You Should Be Sad - Halsey
How Could You Leave Us - NF
The A Team - Ed Sheeran
Animals - Maroon 5
Falling - Harry Styles
Goodbyes - Post Malone ft. Young Thug
Circles - Post Malone
Without Me - Halsey
Playing With Fire – N-Dubz ft. Mr Hudson
Bring Me To Life – Evanescence
My Immortal – Evanescence
Don't Go – Wretch 52 ft. Josh Kumra
Deepest Shame – Plan B
Feel It – Michele Morrone
I See Red (Everybody Loves An Outlaw) – Lali Agazade
You Don't Own Me – SayGrace ft. G-Eazy
Lullaby For A Soldier – Maggie Siff
Cryin' – Aerosmith

Always – Bon Jovi
Hero – Enrique Iglesias
Sex On Fire – Kings of Leon
We Belong Together – Mariah Carey

Chapter 1

ANNA

It's a warm, sunny day. I tip my head back to feel the rays on my face. I love my little garden— it's a sun trap. "Mummy," whispers Malia in my ear.

I smile but keep my eyes closed. "Yes, sweetie?"

"When I was at nursery today, Ziggy asked me to kiss him." My eyes shoot open and fall on the innocent face of my five-year-old daughter. "He wants me to be his . . . " She taps her pink, heart-shaped lips that are the exact replica of my own. "Old lady. What does that mean?"

"You are far too young to be kissing anyone, little miss," I say, and she giggles. "I hope you told him that." She shrugs her shoulders and the pink strap of her dungarees slips down. "Sweetie, I really wish you'd make some new friends. You and Ziggy spend an awful lot of time together and it's important that you make other friends."

"But I only like Ziggy and he only likes me," she says innocently.

I hear the front door open and close. "I brought cakes for little miss trouble and wine for us to get started," yells Eva from inside the house. "You better have your ass in that shower," she adds. I check my watch. *Christ, is it that time already?* I push myself to stand and brush the grass from my ass as I sweep Malia into my arms and take her inside.

"Sorry, I lost track of time," I explain. "I'm going right now. You look amazing, by the way."

Eva always looks amazing. An inch taller than me, she stands at five-foot-three, and her slim build and shoulder-length brown hair make her a natural beauty. Her green eyes sparkle, giving the impression she is always happy. She's wearing the light blue denim jeans she purchased for over a hundred pounds on our last shopping trip and a white top that shows off her midriff.

I shower quickly and dress in a thigh-length summer dress. It's flowy from the waist down and looks perfect with my heeled boots. I apply minimal make-up and get downstairs just as Eva's mum arrives. "Thanks for watching Malia, Esther. She's been excited since she came home from nursery today," I say with a smile. As if to prove my point, Malia races into the hallway and throws herself into Esther's arms.

"It's not a problem. You know I love to spend time with her. Now, come and tell me what things you and Ziggy have been up to this week," says Esther fondly as she carries Malia into the living room.

Eva passes me my clutch bag and smiles. "Ready?" she asks. I nod. I've been ready for this night out since she mentioned it last week. I go and kiss Malia on the head and repeat the rules of bedtime so she doesn't try anything with Esther. They smile at each other mischievously and I already know they plan on staying up past bedtime.

We often drink local to where we live. I'm new to this area, but Eva's lived here for years. As usual, we start at The Duke. It's a pretty lively bar. We have to queue for our drinks, and then there's nowhere to sit, so we find ourselves finishing the first drink pretty quickly so we can move on to somewhere less lively.

As it happens, most of the bars along Queen's Road are busy, and by the time we stumble into The Copper Trap, we're both feeling the alcohol buzz. The staff here know us well and our drinks are already on the bar before we've asked for anything. I smile gratefully at Cathy, the head bartender, and we take our drinks to a quiet corner. I fill Eva in on what Malia said about Ziggy. She finds the whole thing hilarious. "You're overreacting. He's just a kid too and probably doesn't understand what he's saying," she reasons.

"That's bullshit. His dad is a biker. He wears the leather jacket with the thingy on the back," I say.

"The club badge?" asks Eva.

"Whatever it is," I dismiss. "One of the other mums at school told me it's a gang. He's basically in a biker gang and his kid is out of control."

"You know you shouldn't believe everything you hear. Do you think the same mum said nice things about you when she found out who Malia's dad really was?" she asks, raising a perfectly plucked brow at me. I scowl, but she continues regardless. "You know more than anyone not to listen to gossip because it's usually wrong."

I scoff. "The gossip doesn't do Reggie justice. He's way worse than any story. Besides, I'm pretty sure none of the parents at Malia's school know about Reggie being her dad."

Eva smirks. "Yeah right. Sounds like they love to gossip, if you ask me." She sighs. "If you're really worried, then speak to the teacher. Maybe she can try and encourage Malia to play with different kids, but I really think she'll be heartbroken without Ziggy. She's really taken with him." I roll my eyes. Eva is a hopeless romantic.

"If we have to move again, they'll be two very sad kids. They shouldn't get so attached. Don't you think it's weird to be this attached at their age? Maybe I should go straight to his dad and tell him what his kid's been saying?" I suggest. "Ask him to speak to Ziggy about making new friends?"

Eva shakes her head. "Oh, I don't think that's a good idea." But my mind is made up and the alcohol makes me slightly braver than I'd normally feel. I drain my drink and stand. Eva looks panicked. "You mean now?" she whisper-hisses and I nod.

"His gang drinks at The Windsor."

"Please stop calling it a gang. It's not how they like to be seen. It's a club, and if you call it a gang, he might get mad," says Eva with a hint of hysteria in her voice.

We walk to The Windsor pub and stand outside. It doesn't look anything special, just like a regular bar. Nobody ever goes in there unless they are part of the bike gang. It's a fact everyone just seems to know without anyone having to say it.

A few men are standing around outside chatting and smoking cigarettes. Eva grabs my arm. "I think this is a very bad idea," she whispers.

"It's fine. He's hardly gonna kill us for being concerned parents."

"Actually, you're the concerned parent. I said I wasn't concerned at all. In fact, I laughed and told you it was nothing to worry about. I want it noted that I laughed." She's stressing out. Eva hates confrontation, and usually, I'd avoid it too, but alcohol makes me brave.

I smile and untangle her arm from my own. "Noted."

I lead us towards the entrance and a beefy arm shoots out, blocking our path. "Who are you?" he grunts, and I step back slightly to see a mountain of a man with dark eyes and a ruddy face.

"Who are you?" I ask and he glowers at me through slits that look nothing like eyes anymore.

"Are you trying to be funny?" he growls, his forehead creasing with a frown."Nope. It's only right that you introduce yourself first because you want to know who I am." He stares at me, completely baffled, and then I hear Eva sigh as she pushes forward.

"Sorry. My friend forgot her manners. I'm Evalyn and she's Anna." His eyes seem to soften at Eva as he assesses her. "We're just here to have a quick chat with, erm . . . " She looks at me seemingly for a name, but I shrug my shoulders. Her eyes widen. "You mean you dragged me here and you don't even know who the hell you're looking for?" she whisper-hisses.

"I've never spoken to him," I hiss back. "I didn't know it was the kind of place to have a fucking guest list. It's a dump."

"Oh wow." She throws her hands up in the air and turns to face me. "Are you trying to see how many insults you can throw at this poor man before he escorts you away from the premises?"

I notice we now have the attention of some of the other men. "I'm just saying that—" I begin.

"Forget it," the mountain utters. "You're both driving me nuts. Go, look inside for whoever it is you want. What harm can you pair do? I'll give you two minutes before I come and kick your asses out." He steps to the side and Eva gives me a triumphant smirk before leading us inside.

"Good cop-bad cop never fails," she says, looking around the crowded bar. "Shit, are they having sex?" she asks. Her eyes practically pop out of her head. I follow her stare over to the snooker table and realize that, yes, there's a couple having sex, and nobody is taking the slightest bit of notice.

"Christ, let's hurry up and get out of here." I take her arm and pull her through the bar. I've never seen so many men wearing the same leather jacket before. It makes it harder to spot the man I want, but when I do, he takes my breath away. It's not the first time that's happened. When I first saw him at the school gates, I thought my panties would melt off and jump in his pocket. They were desperate to come off. He doesn't come to the school often, so I don't get to appreciate his hotness on a daily basis.

He throws his head back and a deep, rumbling laugh escapes his gorgeous mouth. His tall, six-foot something frame is well-hidden with him sitting on a barstool, but I've got that silhouette burned into my brain. His broad shoulders and bulging arms are covered in tattoos and there's something about his light blue eyes that gives him a permanently smouldering look. Eva nudges me forward and I realize I'm standing still, just staring at him.

"You know he's staring right back at you wondering what the fuck you're gawking at, right?" she whispers into my ear. I swallow the dry lump in my throat and move closer to him. The guys he's with also turn to stare at us, and I'm pretty sure the conversation in this place just dropped down to almost whispering.

"Hi," I croak, and he stares at me blankly. I didn't expect him to remember me. He's probably never paid any attention to us mere mortals who lust after him at the playground. In fact, I think in the whole three months Malia's been going to that nursery, I've seen him three times max. "I'm Malia's mum."

"Shit, Pres, she ain't about to drop a kid on you, is she?" asks one of the men, laughing.

"Shut the fuck up, Tiny," mutters Ziggy's dad. "Lady, what do you want?"

My mouth opens and closes a few times. *What did I want again?* "Malia," Eva whispers into my ear to give me the reminder I was silently begging for.

"Malia," I blurt out. He begins to look annoyed. "She plays with Ziggy."

A look of realization passes over his face and he stands up. I hear Eva gasp at his sheer size.

"What did he do?" he asks.

"Nothing," I say, shaking my head back and forth. "I think they should have other friends," I blurt out. I'm getting this all wrong, and he studies me silently for a few seconds. He's understandably confused by my ramblings.

"Come," he says and sighs. He takes me by the hand, and I stare down in awe at how his giant paw covers mine completely. He pulls me through the bar to a quiet table away from the crowd of bikers. I look back at Eva. One of the other men is talking to her as she looks over at me helplessly. Ziggy's dad practically shoves me to sit down at the table and then lowers himself opposite me. "Start talking."

"Ziggy and Malia always play together. Today, he asked her to kiss him," I blurt out. "He wants her to be his old lady?" I say it as a question because I'm not quite sure what that part means but I'm guessing marriage. He laughs— really laughs, throwing his head back again. If it wasn't at my child's expense, I'd be mesmerized by the way his throat bobs up and down or the way his tattoos cover up under his chin and are partially hidden by his well-groomed beard.

"Fucking legend." He chuckles, but when he sees I'm not laughing, he coughs to clear his throat and straightens up in his chair. "So, now you don't want them to play together?"

"No," I say firmly. "I think they should make other friends."

He nods his head slowly. "Because my kid's not good enough for yours?"

"I didn't mean . . . it's just that . . . " I'm stuttering helplessly.

"Oh, I know what you meant. My kid's not good enough to play with Reggie Miller's daughter," he sneers. At the mention of Reggie's name, I begin to breathe faster, the colour draining from my cheeks. I grip the edge of my chair to stop me from running out of here. "You thought I didn't know who my kid was hanging out with? Oh, I know. I know everything. So, while you stand in that playground with your head up your ass, I know all about you and Reggie and the things he's done." He leans back and folds his arms over his chest. "Now, you listen to me, lady. I'm not overjoyed by my kid's choice in friends either, but for some reason, he worships your daughter, and unlike you, I trust him to make his own decisions. You want to break your kid's heart, then be my guest. Now, get the fuck outta my bar."

I stand on wobbly legs, hardly believing that he's speaking to me like this when he doesn't even know me. I turn to walk away but then something takes over me.

I vowed never to be walked all over again, so I find myself turning to face him. "I wanted them to make other friends because I have to move a lot thanks to Reggie. But I'm sure you knew that already. I thought it wouldn't be very good for your son to be so invested in my daughter because when we have to leave again, he'll be heartbroken. I'm glad your son doesn't have your poor manners."

I turn on my heel and march over to Eva. She smiles, looking relaxed, and hands me a drink. "We have to leave," I say.

"No, come and meet Rock." She smiles. The man who stopped us earlier at the door offers a goofy grin. "And Lake," she adds, pointing to the man at Rock's side. "We've put some money in the jukebox. Rock love's rock music," she states proudly and then falls into a fit of giggles brought on by the alcohol.

"Eva, we really need to leave."

I feel him approaching. It's like a sensation washes over me and I have to fight the urge to shudder. I feel the heat of his body against my back, and when he leans closer to my ear, I gasp.

"You're a feisty little thing," he whispers.

"I'm leaving. I'm just trying to get my friend to say goodbye to these gentlemen and then we'll be off," I explain.

"No rush," he mutters. "Stick around. Maybe I was a little harsh back there."

"See, he said we can stay." Eva smiles and holds out her hand for him to shake. "I'm Eva, Anna's best friend."

"Riggs," he answers. I realise this is the first time I've heard his name. He didn't bother to introduce himself back there. Even the mums at the playground refer to him as 'Ziggy's dad'.

"Ziggy's cute," she compliments, and this seems to ease the annoyance that surrounds Riggs' eyes. "I only met him a couple of times. Malia adores him."

A realization passes over Rock's face. "You two are together?" he asks, running his finger between me and Eva. "Like in a relationship?"

"No." Eva laughs. "We're not lesbians."

"Rock, this one's Reggie Miller's woman," says Riggs. My face instantly goes a deep shade of red with embarrassment. Eva feels the anxiety radiating from me at the mere mention of my ex.

"I'm not his woman," I utter.

"Oh yeah," Rock says with a grin. "And he knows you're drinking in these parts, does he?"

"I'm not his woman," I repeat.

"Maybe we should go," says Eva, grabbing hold of my hand.

"Better still, let me call him. I'm sure he'd love to hear from me," says Rock, pulling out his cell. My hand dashes towards it, snatching it away from him. I'm shaking from fear and panic. Rock's mouth falls open, not quite believing what I just did, which makes two of us.

"He doesn't know I'm here," I mutter. "You can't tell him that you saw me."

Rock moves closer and my fear deepens. "I'll tell him whatever I like. He ain't shit around here."

I glance at Riggs, who's smirking at the interactions unfolding before him. "Do you let all your gang members talk to women like shit?" I snap.

"It's not a gang, sweetheart. What your boyfriend has is a gang. What I have is a club," says Riggs with ease.

"The only difference I see is this gang wears leather jackets and his gang wears suits," I say boldly.

Riggs grins. "I can name a million differences between my club and Reggie's gang. The first being we don't beat on our old ladies. We treat them like the queens they are."

I scoff and fold my arms across my chest. "Well, clearly you don't respect women because you've spoken to me like shit tonight."

"I said we treat *OUR* old ladies like queens. You're not an old lady. You're Reggie's woman. I don't need to respect you." He pops a cigarette in his mouth. "The last I heard, he beat you so badly, you spent a week in the hospital." He saunters past me and heads for the exit, lighting his cigarette.

"It was a bad idea to come here," mutters Eva. "Let's get out of here."

Chapter 2

RIGGS

I don't know what just came over me. Something about Malia's mum riles every cell in my body. Who the fuck does she think she is turning up in my bar and lecturing me about my kid? Looking down her nose at us? I shake my head and take a long drag on my cigarette.

"She's a firecracker," smirks Lake.

"She's got nerve turning up here like that, thinking I didn't know who her old man is."

"I thought she got an order out on Reggie. He can't go near her these days," says Lake.

"She didn't like being called his woman," I say. "You think she's in this part of town because he can't get to her here?"

The door opens and the two women step out. I stare straight ahead. I know it's her as she passes because I feel her under my skin. "Ass," she mutters under her breath. Lake grins at me and I shake my head again, laughing to myself.

"'Scuse me?" Despite me telling her to get out of my bar, I've actually enjoyed our banter and I'm not quite ready for it to end.

"I said," she grits out, spinning to face me, "that you're an ass."

"I heard," I nod. "Why?"

Her mouth falls open and her eyes widen. "Are you kidding me? I've never met anyone so rude and ... " She pauses, trying to find the right word. "Rude," she repeats.

"Go home. You've drunk too much and you turned up here to discuss your kid. Come back when you're sober and maybe I'll listen to what you have to say."

"Fuck you," she hisses.

"Do you kiss Reggie with that mouth?" Lake smirks.

"Let's just go," says her friend on a sigh. "They'd never understand."

"Understand that a mob princess had the nerve to come here? I understand perfectly." I move towards them, and if I'm not mistaken, Anna has a heated look in her eyes. "Maybe I'll rock up to your place, see what you're like without that alcohol running through your blood." I run my finger down her bare arm. Goosebumps break out on her skin and she sucks in a breath. I smirk.

"I'm not telling you where I live," she mutters.

"I don't need you to. See ya around, sweetheart." I turn back to the guys, grinning with satisfaction. This woman will regret putting herself on my radar.

I take Ziggy's backpack from the kitchen counter. "You're taking him to school?" asks my mum. I note the shock in her voice.

"Yep," I say, not wanting to get into it.

"Yay!" Ziggy grins. "Can we go on the bike?" he asks. I nod and he fist pumps the air.

"No," says my mum firmly. "Finn, you know the school will call and question whether the bike is safe. It isn't worth the bother. Just take my car." She throws the keys and I catch them.

We get into the car and I fasten Ziggy in. "Daddy, why does Granny call you Finn?"

"Because that's my real name," I say. "And because she's my mummy, she's allowed to use that name."

"I like Riggs better," he says.

"You're lucky because you get to call me by a name that nobody else can call me," I say. "Daddy." This satisfies him and he smiles. "Now let's get you to school."

I stand uncomfortably in the playground. I hate the school run because I stand out. All the other adults here are mainly mums and they stare at me cautiously. They pull their kids closer to their sides like they don't quite trust me.

I check my watch again and sigh. There're still five minutes to go. Ziggy suddenly screeches and takes off towards the gates. He crashes into a little blonde and wraps her into a hug. Her little curls bounce from the impact and she giggles. "Malia, my daddy's real name is Finn," he announces, taking her hand and pulling her towards me. "He brought me to school today."

Malia stops in front of me. She tips her head back and stares right at me. She has her mum's light green eyes, which reminds me . . . I glance towards the gate as a harassed-looking Anna bustles in. She has shades covering her eyes and I suspect she's feeling hungover. "Malia," she bristles, and the little girl turns towards her. "I told you not to run ahead," she adds.

The little girl pouts. "But I saw Ziggy," she says in a little voice. "And look! His daddy brought him to school today. He's so big!" I smile down at the little version of Anna.

Anna stands a few feet away and stares at the closed classroom door. Maybe she's willing it to open up, like me. "Sore head?" I ask.

She glances at me and lifts her shades slightly to meet my eyes. I like that she's showing me no fear. "Are you talking to me?" she asks coolly.

I make a show of looking around at the space around us. The other mums are giving me a wide berth. "Looks that way."

"My head is just fine, thank you." Her tone is cold and impatient.

"I thought we could grab a coffee and discuss last night?" I ask.

"I don't think so," she mutters.

"You not so brave now that you're sober?" I ask.

The doors open, and Ziggy's teacher smiles warmly at me. She's had a thing for me for the last year, since Ziggy first started in her class. "Oh, how lovely to see you, Finn." She smiles. "Would you like to stay and look through some of Ziggy's work? He's been doing so well."

"I have a coffee date with Anna," I say, tipping my head in Anna's direction. The teacher straightens slightly and looks Anna up and down.

"He doesn't have a coffee date with me," mutters Anna. Her face flushes red with embarrassment.

"I do," I correct. I hand Ziggy his backpack and he runs inside, pulling Malia with him. I turn to Anna and smile. "You can either walk outta here with me or I can embarrass you in front of all these judgy bitches."

"You wouldn't dare," she growls.

"Oh baby." I smirk. "Please don't wave the red rag. You don't know me well enough to challenge me."

Anna squares her shoulders and glances around at some of the other mums who are kissing their kids goodbye at the door. "Fine," she mutters.

I follow her out of the gates and point her in the direction of a nearby café.

"I don't want a drink," she mutters when the barrister comes to take our order.

"Two coffees," I order, ignoring her eye roll. We sit by the window. "So," I begin, "how are you settling in around here?"

"You haven't brought me here to ask that," she says coldly. "You want to know about Reggie and whether I'm a threat in your part of town. Well, I can tell you that I'm not. I am not with him. He doesn't have my address and I see him very briefly at Malia's supervised visits at a contact centre in central London. Neutral ground to both of you, apparently."

"I guess you went home last night and did some research about my club?" I smile.

"Gang wars aren't hard to research." She sighs.

"You like that word, gang," I point out. "If you'd have done your research properly, you'd know I'm not in a gang."

She looks uninterested and picks at a white paper napkin. "Look, I'm here to get on with my life. I'm not interested in you or your club and I'm not interested in Reggie or any of his dealings. The stuff going on with you and him has nothing to do with me and Malia. I shouldn't have come into your bar last night. It was a stupid move and one I didn't think through properly. I'll probably move again in a month or two, then you'll never see me again and the world will go on turning."

"Why do you move so often?" I ask.

"That's none of your business and I don't want to discuss it with you. All you need to know is I'm no threat to you."

I lean back in the chair as the waitress sets down two coffees. Anna thanks her politely and the smile she radiates is beautiful. I want to see it more. "I don't see Reggie as a threat, Anna. He doesn't concern me and neither do you. You came to me about our kids."

"I was drunk. It was stupid. I'll speak to the teacher about getting them to play with other kids too."

"No. They're happy. Why would you rip them apart? If you leave, then I'll deal with the fallout from Ziggy. It's not your problem. Your kid is used to moving on, so I'm sure she won't ever think of him again. So, why here? What made you move here?"

Anna begins to fiddle again, and I gently place my hand over hers to still her fidgeting. She glances at me and I wonder if she feels the electricity radiating between us too. "It's safe here," she says. "He can't come here without causing himself problems and Reggie doesn't like problems."

"And you said that he doesn't know you're here?" I ask because I find that hard to believe. Reggie will know exactly where she is, especially because his daughter is here too.

"Not yet." She glances around the café. "But he'll find out."

"And then you'll run. How long will you run for?"

"Maybe I won't need to, now that I'm in this part of town?" she shrugs her slender shoulders.

"Why do you run, Anna?" I ask again. "If he sees Malia anyway, then what's the reason for running?"

"He isn't allowed to have my home address because he threatened to kill me. And he will." She stares directly at me. "One day, when I think he's over it, that's when he'll do it. I move and he eventually finds my address and takes great delight in telling me he's found me." A sad look passes over her face. "It's a game to him."

"He's a mob boss. He'll always know where you are," I point out. "He probably knows where you are the second you sign a new lease."

She shrugs. "Maybe. But if I stop playing the game, he'll strike. He'll think I'm complacent." She rubs at her face, and for the first time, I notice how tired she looks. "I don't even know why I'm telling you this. You don't need to know. I should go." She stands. "I'm sorry about last night. It won't happen again."

As I watch her rush off, I'm left thinking of how much I want it to happen again.

When I get back to the clubhouse, I find Cree, my Vice President, sitting in my office. "Lake tells me you met Reggie Miller's wife last night at the bar?" he asks.

I nod and take a seat opposite him at my desk. "What of it?"

"Well, why the fuck was she in The Windsor? In fact, why the fuck is she even in this part of London?"

"I knew she was here, Cree. I didn't see it being an issue. Her kid started at Zig's school about four weeks ago when she moved here."

"And you didn't think that was something you should share?" asks Cree.

"Why? She's split from him. Got an order from the courthouse just last month."

Cree glares at me, the vein in his neck ticking because he's pissed. "You did the research and didn't share. What the fuck, man?"

"Stop bitching," I groan. "It's not important information. Reggie isn't stupid enough to start a war with us. He'll stay over the tracks. Stop worrying."

"So what did she want with you?"

"To talk about our kids. Not everything is club related. Ziggy told her girl that he wanted to kiss her and then he asked her to be his ol' lady. No big deal. I'll talk to Ziggy and that's the end of that."

Cree laughs. "That kid," he says affectionately. "So, this woman isn't a problem for us?"

I shake my head and open my laptop to run a search on Anna Miller. I don't know if she goes by that surname, but when I pop it into the search engine, the screen is flooded with news stories about her attack a few months ago. I click through them, all reporting similar events: *Police and ambulance were called to a domestic incident in which businessman Reginald Miller was involved. His wife was rushed to the hospital where she remains critical.*

I continue to look through the feed. A few later reports confirm Reggie was arrested for the assault of his wife, Anna Miller. The court case was only two months ago, and although Reggie was found guilty, he wasn't imprisoned due to other factors. It doesn't list the factors, but I imagine they involved large sums of money passing hands. It would explain why Anna isn't dead already— the bent judge would have put restrictions on contact.

"Is she as hot as Lake said?" Cree smirks.

I nod my head, still staring at the news story in front of me. "H.O.T.," I spell out. "It's crossed my mind to hit her up."

"Because you fancy her or because it's a reason to get under Reggie's skin?" he asks. I grin. He knows me well, so I don't need to answer that. "You're addicted to trouble," he adds, shaking his head. "She got any H.O.T. mates?" he asks, and I laugh harder.

Chapter 3

ANNA

"He said what?" screeches Eva. "Oh my god." I'd filled her in over the phone all about my coffee this morning with Riggs. "Why does he want to know about Reggie anyway?"

"In case it impacts them, I guess. It won't. Reggie won't expect me to know anything about the boundaries. I had to message Luella and ask her about it," I admit. "She promised she wouldn't tell Stephan that I'd been in contact." Luella is the wife of Reggie's right-hand man. We were close before Reggie and I split.

"Do you still trust her?" asks Eva.

"Yeah," I say. "She helped me out a lot back when I was with Reg. She didn't tell Stephan any of it." I check my watch for the time. "I have to go. I have a job interview at a garage. Just office work, but it'll pay the bills," I say. "And it's temporary, which is ideal if I have to move again. Will you be my reference?"

"You aren't moving again, Anna. I love having you right up the road. And of course, I will. Good luck with the interview. I'll call by on my way home from work and see how you got on."

I enter the garage where there's a man with his head under the hood of a car and another man working on a motorbike. They both look up and the mechanic nearest to me comes out from under the bonnet and wipes his oily hands on a rag. "Can I help you?" he asks.

"I'm Anna. I came about the job."

He smiles and holds his hand out for me to shake. "The name's Gears," he says. "Let's go to the office." He leads me up some metal stairs into an office that overlooks the garage. He pulls out a seat and I sit. "As you can see, I need help," he says, pointing to a stack of papers. "I can't file paperwork away for shit and the boss gets on at me. I can't fix cars and sort paperwork and answer the phone."

"Well, I can definitely help you because I'm great at all of those."

He grins and I hand him my passport. He glances over it. "Can I make a copy?" I nod and he snaps a photo of the passport before handing it back. "I'll need to check you out. You got a previous employer?"

"Yes. You can call Eva Holmes. She employed me as her P.A. for many years," I lie. The truth is Reggie wouldn't let me work and so the only experience I have is from years ago when I first left school. I don't want to complicate things with my past and that's why I have a passport in my maiden name. But I know I can do this job with ease.

"Right, well, leave that with me. I'll give Eva Holmes a call and then I'll let you know. When would you be able to start?" he asks.

"Straight away. I've just moved to the area, so I'm free."

He leans across the desk and we shake hands again. "I'll be in touch."

I practically skip out of there. This is exactly what I need and I'm excited. I know Eva will give me a glowing reference. I decide to treat myself to lunch at the same café where I had coffee with Riggs.

I'm enjoying a fresh leafy salad when my mobile phone rings. I groan when I see Reggie's name, but if I don't answer, he'll just keep calling. "Hello," I say brightly.

"I need to change visitation," he says coldly. "Bring Malia tomorrow."

"I can't bring her tomorrow. Your day is Sunday. You shouldn't be calling me about this stuff, Reggie. Contact the Centre."

"I did that, Anna, and they said if I cancel Sunday, then I'll just have to skip a week unless you call to arrange it. I want to see Malia this week. I just can't do Sunday."

"One week won't hurt. Malia will understand. We'll do it next Sunday instead." I keep my voice light because I don't want to upset him. He's vicious when he's angry.

"Shit, Anna, don't be like this. I need to see her. I've missed her," he says. It's a lie, of course. He insists on seeing her so he can see me. "We can meet up somewhere public so you feel safe." Again, it's a lie. He'd yell at me no matter where we were. We could stand outside the police station and he'd still not give a crap.

"No. That's not a good idea."

I hear his intake of breath. He's getting impatient with me. "I'm not asking you, I'm telling you. Bring her to the usual park, the one she used to love before you took her away from me. After school, tomorrow, or I'll come to your house." I hold my breath because this is the part where he reels off my address and then I panic and move us again.

Before he gets to that part, I sigh. "Right. Fine. I'll be there at four."

"Good," he says, sounding more relaxed.

"But Reggie, I'm bringing someone with me. If you lay a hand on me, they'll call the cops."

"Yeah, yeah, princess," he mutters, his tone bored. "See you tomorrow."

I cut the call and lay the mobile on the table. I've lost my appetite and I push the salad around the plate. "You not eating that?" It's Riggs' deep, rumbling voice and I drop my fork in surprise. It clatters and a few heads turn to see what the fuss is. He stands to the side of my table. Behind him are some of his gang members, who take the next booth.

"I'm not hungry," I mutter.

"Hmm, it looks filling." He smirks.

"I've been in this part of town for almost five weeks," I say. "I didn't bump into you once. I come to see you at the bar and now I see you everywhere."

"You sound annoyed by that," he says. "You're new to town. It's good to make friends."

"You didn't seem too friendly last night when you told me to get the fuck out of your bar," I quip.

"Maybe I was a bit harsh. I get testy when it comes to Ziggy."

One of Riggs' friends approaches us. He's just as tall as Riggs, with the same bulging muscles covered in tattoos. It must be a clause in their gang rules that you can only join up if you're hot as hell. He lowers his shades and I almost gasp out loud when his electric blue eyes meet my own. "And who's this beauty?" he drawls.

"Anna," Riggs says and sighs. "Meet one of my enforcers, Blade." He holds out his hand. His tattoos cover it, making my hand look pale in comparison.

"You weren't kidding when you said she was hot," says Blade, and Riggs shakes his head, laughing.

"It's nice to see you again, Anna. Take care." Riggs shoves Blade back over to where their friends sit.

My mobile phone rings again. I answer the withheld number and smile when it's the garage offering me a two-week trial period to see how we get along. I accept, grateful that I don't have to touch any of Reggie's money.

"You look happy, Angel," says Blade from his spot at the edge of his table.

"Angel?" repeats Riggs.

Blade shrugs. "Yeah, she looks all angelic and shit, don't ya think?"

"You're giving her a nickname?" laughs another of the men at their table. "Shit just got real." Blade and Riggs stare at each other for a few seconds. A look passes between them, then they smile and the moment's gone.

"Goodbye," I say as I gather my bag and jacket. "I'll see you around."

"You certainly will," smiles Riggs with a promise in his eye. "Angel," he adds, grinning at Blade.

I collect Malia from school and I'm disappointed when I notice Ziggy's grandma is there instead of Riggs. I laugh to myself. Why am I even thinking about him? My life's complicated enough and a few harmless flirts doesn't mean he likes me like that. If anything, he probably feels sorry for me. My history with Reggie is enough to put any man off me for life.

Eva is waiting for me when I arrive home. "So?" she asks as I unlock the front door.

"I got a trial," I smile. "Thanks for the reference."

"I mean, it's asking for trouble. I assume Riggs doesn't know."

I frown in confusion. "What are you talking about?"

"The garage. Riggs' club owns it."

I stare open-mouthed. That's new information and I'm suddenly sick with nerves. He'll think I'm stalking him. "No, that can't be right," I groan.

"I checked it out after I spoke to the manager about your reference. It's owned by the Kings Reapers."

"I can't take the job then," I sigh, plonking myself down onto the kitchen table. He's gonna think I'm some crazy lady turning up wherever he is."

"You saw him twice." Eva laughs. She turns the kettle on, then gets Malia a drink of juice from the refrigerator. "That's hardly stalking."

"Three times," I correct her. "He turned up at the café where I went to get some lunch."

Eva fixes me with a stare that makes me blush. "Would that have been the same café where Riggs took you for coffee?" she asks. I nod my head and look away. "Did you go there hoping to see him?"

"No." I gasp and then smile. "I don't think I did. If I did, then it was subconsciously."

"Oh, Anna. You have that look in your eye," she groans. "Stay away from the biker."

"I am. It was a coincidence is all. The chances of me seeing him again are thin. I'll avoid the café and turn the job down."

"You can't turn it down. Maybe he doesn't go into the garage much. He has a manager running things, so do the trial and if, at the end of it, you think it's likely to be an issue, leave," suggests Eva. It sounds like a better plan than turning down a perfectly good job.

"Are you free tomorrow? I need to take Malia to the park near our old house," I say cautiously because I know Eva's gonna spend the next ten minutes lecturing me.

"Why'd ya wanna go there? Reggie or one of his goons might spot you."

I jump down from the table and set about pulling pans out to begin dinner. "Reggie knows. He's gonna be there." I feel her eyes on me. "He can't make the visit on Sunday like planned, so he asked me to meet him tomorrow after Malia finishes school."

"What? Now we're accommodating what Reggie wants?" she snaps.

I take out some potatoes and begin peeling. "I said yes for an easy life. I didn't want him spouting off my new address. It stresses me out and makes me want to move on. I quite like it here."

Eva's eyes soften. "But you know that he knows where you live, Anna. He doesn't have to say the words out loud. He knows the moment you sign for a place."

"But when he says it, it makes it real. If he doesn't, then I can pretend that Malia and I are safe."

"That's crazy," she groans. "It's just words. Being in this part of London makes you a hell of a lot safer than if you were on the other side of the tracks. If you start giving in to his demands, then he'll do it all the time. You're not safe when you're seeing him away from the contact centre."

I nod. I know all this because I've had the same conversation inside my head. The contact centre is monitored. Reggie takes Malia into a room to play and a woman sits in the corner making sure he isn't quizzing her or whatever. It was part of the agreement to keep himself from going to prison.

"Can you come or not? At least if there's someone around, he's likely to behave slightly better." Eva nods, but I can see from the look on her face that she wants to rant some more. I pass her the peeled potatoes and a knife, and she begins chopping. "I'll be okay," I eventually mutter, and she rolls her eyes. "It's just one time. If he does it again, then I'll tell him no."

Chapter 4

RIGGS

"Tell me something," I say, looking Chain's in the eye. "Why is it that every time I look up, you're chatting with my sister?"

Chains shifts uncomfortably and his eyes dart briefly to Cree. "Sorry, Pres. We're just chatting," he says.

I nod slowly. "About?"

"Erm," he stutters before blowing out a puff of air and scratching his head. "All kinds of shit, Pres."

"Sex?" I ask, and he almost chokes.

"Fuck no," he yells. "I wouldn't, Pres. Not with Leia."

"Keep it that way. I don't like the way you eye fuck her. I don't like the way she looks at you either. Just stay the fuck away from her."

Cree laughs as Chains rushes away. We're good mates. Cree, Chains, and I were in the Forces together, but Chains knows how I feel about my younger sister, and he knows that no matter what, he can't ever go there. "You think he fancies Leia?" I grate out.

"Fuck, yes," grins Cree. "I hate to point it out to you, bro, but she's growing up fast. You can't keep her locked up in her ivory tower forever."

"I can. She's nineteen. She doesn't need Chains or any other man in her life." I shake my head and shudder. The thought of seeing Leia with any of my men doesn't sit right.

My mum, Frankie, crosses the clubhouse holding Ziggy in her arms. "Ready?" she asks, and I take my sleepy son from her. It's seven in the evening, almost his bedtime, but some fat arsed judge decided that every two weeks on a Thursday would be the perfect time to force my five-year-old to see his mum.

"As I'll ever be," I sigh. Ziggy doesn't like to go and visit with his mum. He doesn't let me leave him alone with her for the visit, and forcing him to go, even with me there, breaks my heart. Tonight, he's so sleepy that he doesn't bother to argue. I slow the car outside Michelle's run-down place. There's a weaselly-looking guy sitting on the doorstep smoking a cigarette and I groan. The last thing I need is a confrontation with any of her male admirers.

I take Ziggy from his seat and he clings to me. "Will you stay with me, daddy?" he asks, and I kiss his head lightly.

"You bet," I reassure him.

As we get to the door, the weasel looks up. "What?" he grunts. I ignore him and kick the door lightly with my boot because my hands are full with Ziggy. Weasel stands directly in front of me. "I asked you a question," he hisses, and I raise an eyebrow. Ziggy clings tighter and buries his face in my neck.

"You didn't ask me shit. Move," I growl.

The front door opens, and a dishevelled-looking Michelle stands there. Her once bouncy blond curls hang limply, the shine long gone. Her bright blue eyes are dulled by the dark circles under them and her pale skin is almost translucent from lack of sunshine. "Ziggy," she breathes, and I'm grateful she at least sounds happy to see him.

"Michelle," I mutter, stepping around the weasel and heading inside after her. "Did you forget we were coming?" I ask, looking around the stacks of dirty dishes littering the kitchen worktops.

She runs a hand over her hair and smiles weakly. "How have you been, baby?" she asks, moving around my back and trying to catch a glimpse of Ziggy's face. He presses it further into my neck. "Zig?" she whispers sadly.

"Come on, kiddo." I sigh, lifting him so he can't hide his face. "Give mummy a cuddle. She's missed you."

"It's fine if he doesn't want to," she mutters, stepping away. "I get it. How's he been?"

"Good," I say. "School's pleased with his progress. His teacher says he's amazing."

"That's great, Zig," she gushes, and he offers her a small smile. "I'm so proud."

"Are you doing okay?" I ask, looking around at the mess. She does the same.

"Yah know," she shrugs, "I have my good days and bad."

"You need any money or anything? Have you got food?" I ask because, despite my hate for this woman, I can't leave her short.

"I'll be okay. Don't give me cash," she mutters, wincing. "Dave will take it and buy drugs."

"The weasel?" I ask and she gives a small laugh and nods her head. "Do you want me to get rid of him?" I ask.

"No. I like him. He's just got a bad habit is all."

"Should you be around him when you're trying to recover yourself?" I ask and she sighs. "I'm not getting at you, Shell. It can't be easy staying clean if he's not."

"I'm fine. I'll be fine."

"Because you know I won't bring Ziggy if you're using."

"Yes," she snaps. "I know that. Don't nag." The weasel stalks into the kitchen and looks back and forth between us. "Dave, that's Ziggy, my boy." She smiles.

"And him?" he grunts out, pointing at me.

"That's Riggs, Ziggy's dad."

"A biker?" He sneers, and Michelle gives me a pleading look that says to leave it.

"Daddy, can we go, please?" whispers Ziggy. I nod my head and he visibly relaxes.

"Why can't you leave her kid here?" asks the weasel and I glare at Michelle. There's only so much I can take. "She's his mum. He should be here with her," he continues, swaying on his unsteady feet.

"I'll let her fill you in on that," I say dryly as I move to the door. "Next time we come, he won't be here, Michelle," I add, firmly.

"You don't call the shots in my house," he suddenly yells.

I kiss Ziggy on the head and place him outside on the step. "Stay right here, Ziggs. Shout if you get worried, but I just need two seconds with mummy." He nods his head and I turn back towards the kitchen. Michelle groans and buries her face in her hands. "I pay for this house. I pay for the food in it. I furnished it. I own it. I own her. I own that kid. So next time I come around here, you won't be here," I warn.

He squares his shoulders and cracks his neck from side to side. "She's my woman," he growls.

"Then start taking care of her. She's a mess."

"She's exactly how I like her. Get the hell out of my house," he yells.

I crack my fist into his face, feeling satisfied when his nose crunches. Michelle screams and I use my free hand to cover her mouth, tucking her against my side. "Don't scare Ziggy," I whisper calmly. My next hit to his stomach causes the weasel to double over coughing. "Now, don't be a dick or I'll make sure you disappear completely." I pat him on the back and kiss Michelle on the cheek. "Stay clean."

My mum eyes the blood splatter on my t-shirt. "Leia, take Ziggy and put him to bed for me, please," she says, and my sister happily takes Ziggy from my arms. "Talk," she says, pointing to my shirt.

"It was nothing. Some jumped-up asshole shooting his mouth off. Ziggy didn't see a thing."

"Good. He's a sensitive kid. Not like you were at that age." She smiles. "Your dad would have to chase you around the place before you'd listen to a word either of us said. You'd watch the fights break out in this club with a look of awe in your eyes. We knew you'd be just like your dad," she says fondly. I smile. Being like my dad is the biggest compliment anyone could give me. He ran this club well for years until he finally passed from cancer a few years ago. "How was Michelle?" she asks, not bothering to hide the disdain when she says her name out loud.

"Not great. The place was a mess. Can you ask Coral to go over and clean? I'll pay double."

"Finn." She sighs. "Stop doing things for her. You aren't together. If she can't keep her place clean, it's her business."

"Just send Coral over," I repeat. "I want the place cleaned properly and she'll do a good job." Mum nods in agreement, knowing there's no use arguing.

I shower and when I step back into my room, Bonnie, one of the club girls, is lying on my bed. It's the same arrangement each night. She's the only club girl I'll have in my bed. She's clean and I feel comfortable with her, and she doesn't talk shit about my business or gossip with the other whores. "You okay?" She yawns. I nod and slip some shorts on under my towel. "Love it when you're mean and moody," she says and smirks. I throw the sheets back, ignoring her comment, and I climb into bed beside her. I turn my back to her, and she sighs before positioning herself behind me, pressing her body against my own. I close my eyes, exhausted, and I feel myself drifting off almost instantly despite it still being early.

Morning comes around and Bonnie is gone. She usually leaves in the middle of the night. It works for both of us. I dress and head to the room next door to wake Ziggy. By the time we head down for breakfast, my mum is up and busy helping Coral with the cooking. Coral's been around the club for so many years, I can't remember a time before her. Starting as a club whore when my dad was around, she never became anyone's ol' lady, but she stuck around and helps with the club's housekeeping. "I'll take him to school on my way into work," I say. It's rare for me to take Ziggy to school, so twice in one week is a miracle. mum eyes me suspiciously, so I stare down at the newspaper to avoid questions.

I feel her before I see her. A tingling sensation breaks out across my back and then the scent of Anna's fruity perfume fills my nostrils. Ziggy rushes to Malia, just like yesterday. I guess she didn't warn Malia to avoid him after all.

We stand near each other, but I don't look in her direction and she doesn't bother to make conversation. When the classroom door opens, Anna bends down to Malia to kiss her. "Remember, we're seeing daddy after school," she says softly and Malia cheers happily.

A different sensation hits me in the chest, one I haven't felt since I first met Michelle. I don't like that Anna's seeing her ex and I won't be there to check that she's safe. I shake it off quickly. I've no business feeling shit like that.

I follow her out of the school gates. She looks different today, dressed in a tight skirt and matching jacket. "You work?" I ask and then realize too late that it sounds rude.

"Yes."

"Sorry, I didn't mean to be rude. I just thought Reggie wouldn't allow that," I say, and she gives an awkward smile. "I thought he'd give you money." I guess not everyone supports their exes like me.

"Bye," she says quietly and walks away in the opposite direction. Seeing Anna is becoming an addiction. I need to stop turning up where she is. I decide this will be the last time I try to see her. No more school runs. No more café lunches. Nothing good will come of me chasing Reggie Miller's missus.

I go to the gym for my usual workout with Cree and Chains. "You and Bonnie again last night?" puffs Chains, lifting the weights. "What's that, a month at least? Are you taking her as your ol' lady?"

I shake my head. "She's good at sucking cock, what can I say?" I snigger through the lie.

"She's only been around for a couple of months. Why do you always get to test run the whores?" asks Chains.

"Man, don't call them that," I groan. I hate that name being used for the girls who hang around the club. "We don't pay them, so they're not whores."

"Free accommodation. Free food. That's the payment," he points out.

"Don't be bitter. Now, are we working out or are you just gonna talk shit like a bitch?" I ask and he grins.

After the workout, Chains makes some excuse about having to meet a woman to let off steam. How he has steam left after that workout is crazy. Cree and I have other business to attend to, so we head off to The Windsor.

The Kings Reapers purchased The Windsor bar many years ago. I remember running around this place when I was a little kid. Pinky, the woman who runs the bar, is a scary motherfucker. She takes no crap and gives a tonne of it out.

She's cleaning the bar top when we arrive. "He's back there," she says, nodding her head to her living quarters.

Marshall Ankers stands when we enter Pinky's living room. His bodyguard eyes us suspiciously from the corner of the room as we all shake hands. "It sounded important when you called," I begin, taking a seat on the couch opposite to Marshall. Cree moves to the window and stares outside.

"I want to offer you a deal," says Marshall, and I almost snort a laugh. Marshall runs the drugs in my part of town, and I get a good percentage for allowing him to sell on my streets and use my access at the docks to get them into London. There's nothing he can offer me that I can't already take myself.

"Reggie Miller called me. He offered me his streets for a lower percentage than what you take," he continues. Cree turns to face me, but we give nothing away with our expressions. "But Riggs, I hate that motherfucker. There ain't no way I'm working for him. But what if we join sides, me and you?"

I arch an eyebrow and let out a bored sigh. "I thought we were already on the same side, Marshall?"

"We are. I meant what if we team up and sell on his streets too? We could make a fortune. He thinks he'll be getting one over on you, but actually, he won't be." Cree shakes his head at me once to indicate he doesn't like the sound of it. "I'd have to bring more in through the docks, of course, but that shouldn't be a problem, should it?" he asks.

"Ah, so that's the real problem. You need to get a bigger supply into my docks and you can only do that if you bring me on board," I say.

"No, Riggs. The minute he asked me, I rang you to arrange this meet."

"Why is he suddenly trying to get one over on me?" I ask.

Marshall shrugs. "He never said. He rang me out the blue."

"You can tell him to get his own supply. You ain't using my docks."

Once he's gone, Cree takes a seat. "Strange, ain't it," he says, "that Reggie's been quiet for a few months, and now all of a sudden, he's trying to stir up shit. The same week you meet his wife!"

"Coincidence." I shrug. "He's been quiet because he was facing criminal charges for putting his wife in the hospital. That's all done with now, so he's back in the game."

"So what do we do? Ignore that he's trying to take our drug supply?"

I shake my head. "We could get another Marshall like that," I say as I click my fingers. "I'm not worried. But we'll keep a close eye on him just in case he tries to run on both sides of the track. We'll need to call church and warn the brothers. Reggie might approach others who work for us."

My mum calls my mobile as I'm about to head back to the clubhouse for church. "Are you collecting Ziggy today?"

"I've called the brothers back for church. Can you do it?"

She pauses and then lowers her voice. "Actually, I met my friend for lunch and I'm having a nice time. Could you do it?"

"What friend?" I ask, confused by her secretive tone.

"Can you do it or not, Finn?" she asks.

"Jesus, are you with a man?" I gasp and Cree turns to look at me. 'mum', I mouth, and he looks just as shocked as me. "Who the hell is it?"

"I wish I hadn't called," she mutters. "Forget it."

"No," I rush in before she can hang up on me. "I'll get Ziggy. Enjoy your late lunch and don't have unprotected sex. Who knows where he's been if he's as old as you," I joke.

Cree heads back to the club and I detour to get Ziggy. I spot Anna in the playground and stand beside her. She fidgets nervously. "I hate visit nights too," I say, and she glances at me. "I heard you tell Malia about seeing her dad tonight after school," I admit. "Ziggy sees his mum every second Thursday."

"Right," she says. "He changed the day. It's usually on Sundays."

"You said before it was at a contact centre?" I ask.

She nods. "Not tonight, but usually."

"Not tonight?" I ask. "Where are you meeting him tonight?"

"In a park. It'll be busy. It always used to be busy when the weather was nice, and my friend's coming too."

A strange feeling passes through me and sits heavy in my stomach. If this was Leia, I'd never allow this visit to happen. If visiting is at a contact centre, then that shit's for a reason, but I don't know Anna well enough to make demands. Instead, I take her mobile from her hand and input my number. I call my phone so that I also have hers, just in case. "If you need anything, call me."

I hand her mobile back and she smiles gratefully. "Thanks."

Chapter 5

ANNA

I'm six minutes late. Six minutes to Reggie is a long time. I rush through the park and spot him sitting on a wooden bench across from the play area. His men stand amongst the trees surrounding the park, protecting him. "Sorry, the traffic was terrible," I say as we get closer.

"Daddy," screams Malia, throwing herself into his arms. He catches her and smothers her in kisses.

"I missed you so much," he grins. "You and mummy." I shift uncomfortably. I hate it when he says things like that. "Sit down, I don't bite," he adds.

"Actually," I mutter, pulling my Kindle from my bag, "I was gonna cop a spot under the trees and let you two have some time."

"Actually," he mimics, "you'll sit down here."

I glance back to where Eva is sitting across the park and then I take a seat. "Can I go on the slide?" asks Malia.

"Of course, baby. We'll be right here," says Reggie. Malia rushes off happily. Reggie rolls up the sleeves on his expensive shirt. It's a deliberate act to unsettle me because it's something he would do back when we were together, right before he hit me. I bite my inner cheek to stop myself from reacting. "You're looking all smart there, Anna. Did you dress for me?"

I glance down at my grey pencil skirt. "I had to meet Malia's teacher today. Nothing important, but I hate them judging me," I lie. "Malia is doing really well at school."

"I know how my daughter is doing in school. I wish you'd reconsider putting her into a private school. Pilgrims Way Primary School," he shudders. "The name says it all."

I force myself to remain calm. I knew this would happen. It isn't a shock, so why is my heart racing? "Malia," he shouts, and she rushes back. "Mummy tells me she saw your teacher today. Was it good news?"

Malia looks at me confused. "My teacher was sick today, mummy," she says with concern.

"Good girl. Go back and play," says Reggie calmly. My palms begin to sweat, and I rub them along my pencil skirt. I fix my eyes on Eva. She'll call the cops if anything happens, but I've broken the court order by agreeing to see Reggie away from the contact centre, so I'm not sure if that means I'm unprotected legally. Sickness fills my stomach and I bite my cheek harder to stop the rise of bile. "How dare you fucking sit here and lie to my face," he growls. "You think I don't know when you lie?"

"I had a job interview," I lie again. "I didn't get it."

"You don't need a job, Anna. I put enough money into our bank account for you to live on."

"I know," I say quietly. "Thank you." It makes me sicker to be nice to a man I hate more than I've ever hated anything in my entire life.

Reggie runs a finger along my thigh and settles his hand on my knee. "I miss you. I can't ever forgive myself for what I did to you, but I want the chance to put it right."

"No, Reggie." I keep my voice firm and I'm proud of how strong I sound. "Are you going to spend some time with your daughter?"

Reggie grips my chin between his thumb and index finger, and I wince when he forcibly turns my head to face him. "I love you. I want you and Malia to come home. You've made your point and I think I've been quite reasonable to sit by while you dragged me through the courts. That judge cost me a lot of money. It's time for you to come home now." He pushes his lips against mine and his tongue snakes into my mouth. I shove him hard in his chest and he releases me. "Shit, Anna. What's the problem?" he asks.

I stand and step away from him. "The problem is that I don't love you. We will never get back together. If you can't make it to the contact centre in the future, then you'll have to wait because I can't meet you like this again."

When Reggie stands too, my mind races with thoughts—run, yell, scream. Yet I don't do any of those things because fear grips me, and when Reggie wraps his arm around me to turn me away from any onlookers, I close my eyes and prepare myself for the blow. His free hand goes to my throat. It isn't a rushed, spur of the moment move. It's slow and meticulous. His fingers splay out and he presses, adding pressure little by little until I'm gasping for breath. I rake at his arm to try and remove his hand, but it's no use. He eases the pressure and I gasp right before he kisses me again. This time, he catches my lower lip in his teeth and bites until I taste the metallic tinge of blood. "I love the house. The garden is just how you like it," he whispers against my lips. "A sun trap. You should fix the fence panel out back, though. What if Malia gets out?"

He smirks and then goes to Malia in the play area. I rush over to where Eva sits, and she removes her shades. "Are you bleeding?" she gasps. I nod and sit next to her. I find a tissue in my bag and press it to my lip, trying to blink away the tears that threaten to fall. "What the fuck happened? I was watching the whole time," says Eva.

"He's sneaky," I mutter. "I should have listened to you. It was a bad idea to come."

"Yah think?" she hisses. "Fuck, he's crazy."

My mobile rings and I answer without checking the caller I.D. My eyes are fixed on Malia and Reggie. Riggs' voice rumbles 'Hello' and I burst into tears. "Fuck, Anna, what's going on?" he growls.

"I'm fine. Oh god, I'm so . . . " I sniff. "Sorry . . . I don't know . . . why I'm . . . crying," I stutter.

"Are you hurt? Tell me where you are," he demands, and I smile even though he can't see me.

"Honestly, I'm fine. I think my nerves have caught up with me. Thank you for calling, though. It's really sweet."

"I ain't ever been called sweet before," he grumbles. "But I'm glad you're okay."

"Thank you. Maybe I'll see you on the school run tomorrow?" I ask and I don't bother to disguise the hope in my voice.

"Maybe," he replies. "I gotta go. Take care, Anna." The way he says my name in that deep voice sends my stomach into knots.

"Goodbye, Riggs."

I disconnect the call and Eva stares at me open-mouthed. "Riggs has your number?"

"He heard me tell Malia about the contact visit and when I told him it wasn't in the centre, he put my number in his phone. It was nice of him, no?"

"And then he called to check up on you? Wow." Eva fans her face and pretends to faint dramatically.

"Stop," I laugh, shoving her gently. "Our kids are friends, that's all."

I straighten up as Reggie approaches us with Malia in his arms. I hate the feeling of dread that comes over me whenever he's near me. "Be a good girl for mummy," he says, gently kissing her on the head and placing her on the ground. "Maybe I'll come and see your new house," he adds.

Malia smiles wide. "Can you, daddy? I'll show you my bedroom. Mummy painted a princess on my wall."

"Would that be okay with mummy?" asks Reggie, glancing at me with a smug smirk on his face. Malia watches me expectantly. He wants me to be the bad guy.

"We'll see, sweetie," I say. "But remember when we had that talk about daddy not living with us anymore?" I ask and she nods her head. "Well, until the judge tells us that it's okay, daddy isn't allowed to visit our house." The smug smile vanishes from Reggie's face. Maybe he thought I wouldn't explain our new situation to Malia. I'm glad I've surprised him. "Now, kiss daddy goodbye. You can see him next Sunday at the contact centre."

"It's Friday night. A few drinks to celebrate your new job is a great idea," says Eva and I roll my eyes. She turned up at my house dressed for a night out and she's spent the last half hour asking me to go with her. "My mum wants to have Malia over. Don't be mean by denying her the only grandchild she is ever likely to have."

I laugh. "You'll have kids one day and see how tiring it is and then you'll remember this point and see that I said no for a damn good reason."

"Fine, confession time," she mutters. "I've been asked to go out for a few drinks with a guy I met at work. I don't want to go alone."

"That doesn't make me want to go. In fact, it makes me more determined not to."

"Oh come on, Anna. You're young, free, and single. Staying in on a Friday night isn't healthy." There's a knock at the door and I scowl at Eva as she rushes to answer it. She returns with Esther.

"Oh my god, you asked your mum before I'd even agreed!" I gasp and Esther laughs.

"You know how she is when she gets an idea into her head. I was going to take Malia to my house for a sleepover," she says brightly.

"See, babysitter sorted. No excuse. Now, get changed."

We're sitting in the corner of The Duke and I'm filling her in about the things Reggie said to me earlier today. My lip is bruised and cut, and my neck is adorned with finger marks. It's been a few months since I've had to deal with injuries.

Eva smiles happily at something behind me. I turn and see a tall, handsome man in a suit walking toward us. With him is another guy who looks similar in size, tall and medium built. He stops by our table and Eva rises to her feet gracefully and he kisses her on the cheek. "This is my friend, Anna," she says, and I smile weakly, realizing she's set me up on a double date. "Anna, this is Chris. He's an accountant."

"Great to meet you, Anna. Eva told me so much about you. This is my friend, Jamie," says Chris. I offer a little wave and Jamie settles into the seat next to me. "Eva, shall we go to the bar and get the drinks?" asks Chris. I kick her hard under the table and she cries out. I scowl at her to try and communicate that she is not to leave me alone with this stranger, but she smiles sweetly and follows Chris to the bar while rubbing her shin.

"So," smiles Jamie, "Chris tells me you're single."

"Yes. It's hard to get any man who's interested in a twenty-four-year-old with a five-year-old child," I smile back.

"Oh, I love kids," he gushes, and I inwardly groan. He proceeds to tell me stories of his sister's five children and I realize he isn't going to be put off easily.

Eva returns from the bar and she and Chris take over the conversation, which I'm thankful for. I know I'm being a party pooper, but I hate that she sprung this on me. My mobile flashes and it's a text message from Riggs. I smile as I read it.

Riggs: How are you?

I type back that I've been dragged on a double date.

Riggs: Ouch. Have you tried telling him about Malia? Responsibility is a deal-breaker for some men.

I smile again before replying.

Me: Yep, tried that. He loves kids! Eugh!

Riggs: You want me to call and pretend to be from the sexual disease clinic?

I laugh and Eva glares at me. "Something funny happening that you wanna share?" she asks. I shake my head and place my phone back in my bag, feeling like a chastised child.

We're two bottles of wine into the double date when Eva follows me into the bathroom. "What do you think?" she grins.

"They're nice." I shrug. "But Jamie isn't really my type, is he?"

"What, nice and friendly?" she asks. "You need to relax and enjoy it. He's doing all the talking and you're just mumbling answers. Make an effort." She sighs.

"I don't want to, Eva. You shouldn't have set the date up in the first place. I'm not ready to get into another relationship."

Eva stares into the mirror and wipes stray makeup from under each eye. "Who said anything about a relationship? It's a drink with a kind guy, and I bet if Riggs walked in here and asked you on a date, you'd be dragging him up the aisle in no time, screw dating."

"I would not." I blush and she laughs. "I'll try and be nicer," I add. "Just for you." Eva kisses me on the cheek and we head back to the guys.

I check my phone and see another text from Riggs.

Riggs: Which delightful restaurant did your kid loving date take you?

Me: Not that kind of date. No food. Just wine. Eva told me off for being on my phone. Stop distracting me from trying to put my date off of me.

"I think we should try the Cross Keys bar," I catch Eva saying. "It's livelier and there's music."

We agree and finish up our drinks. As we walk to the next bar just a few doors up, Jamie drapes his coat over my shoulders in an attempt at chivalry. It's sweet and I smile gratefully even though I'm not cold.

The Cross Keys is busy. There's a country vibe filling the room and I spot a singer on the stage strumming on his guitar. The dance floor is alive with people having a go at country style dancing. I'm smiling at the scene when someone's hands go to my waist and a deep voice growls, "Excuse me." I shiver and my heart rate triples when I look up into Riggs' eyes. He winks and carries on past me towards the bar like we're strangers.

Jamie's arm snakes around my waist and he leads me to a small table by the dance floor. All four of us squish around it and then the guys decide to go to the bar to get the drinks.

I spot Riggs carrying a tray of drinks. He passes our table without glancing in our direction and sets the tray on a booth table not far from where we are. I recognize a couple of the men from the first night when I went into their bar. A group of women dance nearby and it's clear they are all here together. "Is that Riggs?" asks Eva, and I nod. "They all look like damn models," she adds. "You think it's a requirement to join their club?"

"Probably. I haven't seen one ugly Kings Reaper yet. My first day at the garage was spent drooling at every guy that came in."

"And you didn't see Riggs there?"

I shake my head. "Nope. I met loads of Reapers though, and at one point, I think I actually gasped out loud. Seriously, they are like heaven on a bed of Ben and Jerry's ice cream. I actually wanted to lick each and every one of them to see if they tasted as good as they looked."

Eva laughs. "I'll have to meet you for lunch one day. I need to see some hot ass men."

"Are you saying Chris isn't a hot ass man?" I quip and she laughs. We both know Chris and Jamie are not on the same hotness scale as any of the Kings Reapers.

Jamie is telling me about the time his nephew blew spaghetti out of his nose when my phone pings. I glance over at Riggs and find him staring at me with his mobile in his hand. I try to suppress my smile as I read the message.

Riggs: Try and look interested in what he's saying. You're being rude!

Me: I am interested. His nephew sounds like a hoot. He really does love kids. I'm slightly worried that it's a little too much. I think he's looking for his next baby mumma.

Riggs: You don't want any more kids?

I glance over and see a female rubbing up against Riggs with her arms wrapped around his neck. She's part of his group. When he looks up at her, she plants a kiss on his lips, and he smiles and tucks his phone into his pocket. He wraps his arm around her waist, and I feel disappointment creep in as I look away. It's silly to feel like this— he can kiss who he likes. It's obvious he's just being friendly towards me. I put my phone away and try to focus on the conversation between Chris and Jamie about a football game.

The night progresses to shots. Eva places the tray of eight tequila shots on the table and I catch Riggs' eye. The girl he kissed is sitting on his lap, chatting animatedly to another girl from the group. He smiles at me and I pretend not to notice as I knock the first shot back. My mobile buzzes.

Riggs: Be safe. You're knocking back tequila and you don't know these guys?

I don't reply. Instead, I place my mobile on the table. Riggs watches me as I drink the second shot, and this time I stare back.

Riggs: Everything okay?

Me: Doesn't your girlfriend mind you texting other women?

I watch for his response. He laughs to himself and shakes his head before putting his mobile away.

"Earth to Anna," smiles Eva, waving her hand in front of my face to get my attention. "Do you want to dance?" I let her take my hand and pull me to the dance floor. I keep my back to Riggs and his group. They're getting louder and more boisterous and I don't want to get caught staring at him. "Have you seen that girl all over Riggs?" asks Eva and I shake my head. "She's so pretty. Did he say he had a girlfriend?"

"No, we haven't spoken that much, so why would he?" I shrug casually. Eva gives me a knowing smile. "What?" I ask innocently.

"You fancy him," she accuses. "I mean, I get it, he's gorgeous."

"I think most women would fancy him. Doesn't mean I want to run off into the sunset with him," I say.

"But since Reggie, you haven't shown interest in anyone. It's nice to see that sparkle in your eye when you look over at him."

"The trouble with you, Eva, is you're a hopeless romantic yet you never put yourself out there either," I point out. She's never had a serious boyfriend. A few one-night stands and casual flings, but nothing that ever lasted.

"Excuse me, you see my date there, right? I put myself out there and I just never meet Mister Right."

I feel arms wrap around my waist from behind and try to hide my disappointment when I see that it's Jamie. He holds me close and I fight the urge to shrug him off. Eva leans close to my ear. "Oh my god, you should see the fire in Riggs' eyes right now. He does not like seeing Jamie all over you," she whispers.

"Don't be ridiculous. Riggs has a girlfriend and he really doesn't look at me as anything more than Malia's mum. You're conjuring up scenarios that aren't real," I insist. Eva takes my hand and spins me away from Jamie. I find myself looking at Riggs, and Eva is right, his stare is somewhere between hot and molten. If he could melt Jamie away with just that look alone, he would.

Jamie moves closer and places his hands on my cheeks. I pray quietly that he isn't making a move here on this busy dance floor. In my head, I silently beg him to stop moving his face towards me, and I shudder as his lips brush my own. I step back and Jamie opens his eyes. We stare at each other, not knowing what to say. The moment is awkward and then he smiles, which comes across more like a grimace. "I think I read that wrong," he mutters.

"Sorry," I mutter. "I just don't really see us like . . . that."

Chapter 6

RIGGS

Bonnie takes the cash and heads to the bar to get another round of drinks. My eyes are firmly fixed on Anna. I've enjoyed our little flirty glances and texts, but she seems to have gone cold on me. The blind date guy moves in to kiss her and Anna goes rigid. Her tiny fists curl and she pulls her head back slightly, like she's trying to avoid his lips. It's awkward to watch, but I feel satisfied when she pulls away.

Since vowing to stop myself turning up wherever she is, I've actually seen her more. It's an epic fail on my part. I'd even convinced the guys to come to this bar for a few drinks saying that I liked the live band. It was bullshit— I've never heard of this band, but I hoped that Anna would come here. The strip of bars along this street is where everyone seems to come.

Blade gets a call. "Pres, Cree is at The Windsor. He wants to know when we're going back there."

"One more drink and we'll head back," I say, and he relays it as Bonnie sets the tray on the table. She's been glued to me all evening. I can't exactly tell her to fuck off when she spends every night in my bed. It's easier than explaining to the guys why I blow hot and cold with her.

I spot that the two men who were with Anna and her friend have gone, So I head over to their table. Her friend spots me and she taps Anna. Her perfume fills my nostrils and when she turns to look at me with those big green eyes, I feel like I've been punched in the gut. She's stunning. "We're gonna head back to The Windsor," I say. "You wanna come?" Anna glances back to her friend, who nods her head in response. "Great. Drink up."

"Won't your girlfriend mind?" asks Anna, blushing.

I smirk. It's cute that she's trying to sound casual and unaffected. "Drink up," I repeat, purposely not answering her again.

As we walk back to The Windsor, Anna and her friend trail behind the rest of us, so I wait by the door for them to catch up. She smiles when she sees me waiting and we walk in together. My chest swells with pride. Having her on my arm feels good.

Cree hands me a bottle of beer and then his eyes fall to Anna. "Anna, this is Cree, my VP," I introduce.

"Anna?" repeats Cree, his eyes burning into me. "*Thee* Anna?"

"And this is her friend," I say, ignoring him. He looks at her friend and nods his head in a cool move that he uses when he likes what he sees.

"Eva," she says, holding her hand out for him to shake. He frowns at her offering and then shakes it.

"What happened to your dates, ladies?" I ask.

"Anna upset Jamie, so they left," says Eva. "I was having a nice time," she points out.

"For goodness sake, they were annoying and boring. He tried to kiss me after boring me half to death with stories about his sister's kids," says Anna.

"I thought you'd like a man who likes kids seeing as you have one!" Eva points out.

Anna laughs and her head lifts slightly. I catch a glimpse of a mark on her skin and frown. Then I notice a bruise under her lip and a cut. I take her chin in my hand and tip her head back to get a better look at her neck. When she realizes what I'm doing, she shakes me off. "Are those bruises?" I ask.

"It's nothing," she mutters.

"That's why you were crying when I called you?" I growl.

"Leave it," she says quietly, and Eva gives her a sympathetic smile. It's none of my business, but it's pretty obvious this has something to do with Reggie. I clench my jaw and take a calming breath.

There's a commotion at the door that distracts me, and I spot Rock trying to block someone from getting in. I catch a glimpse of the blond and know instantly that it's Michelle. "Fuck me," I groan. I pass my beer to Cree and head over. "What are you doing here?"

She looks like she's been crying. "Sorry to just turn up like this," she mumbles. "I lost my key. I can't get into the house." She stumbles and I catch her.

"Where's the weasel?" I ask.

"He left," she mutters and begins to cry. "Why can't I keep a man? Why don't they want me?" I look back over to where Cree is chatting with Anna and Eva. I want to spend some time with Anna and now I have to deal with this. I spot the club prospect and grin in his direction. We call him Tiny even though he's at least six-foot-four. He shakes his head, but as a prospect, it's his job to do anything we ask him. "Come on, Pres," he moans. "I have the promise of club pussy tonight."

"I need you to take Michelle back to my room at the club. Don't let my mum see her." I hand her to him, and he sighs heavily. "And lock the door. I don't want her near Ziggy." He nods his head and guides her from the bar.

"She okay?" asks Cree when I return, and I nod. "Where's Tiny taking her?" he asks. I glare at him and he gets the message. I don't want to discuss my ex in front of Anna.

"Let's talk," I say firmly to Anna, leaving her no room to argue. I guide her over to the same table where we sat when I first spoke to her.

"Is this your private table?" she asks. "It's just this place is so busy and this table is always free."

"It was my dad's table," I say fondly. "People don't sit here out of respect."

"Because he was part of your gang too?" she queries. I step closer and back her into the corner of the room.

"Club, Anna," I smirk. "It's an MC club. We have rules and respect. Calling us a gang implies we're like the street rats who sell drugs to kids. A bit like your ex's gang," I say. "Speaking of your ex . . ." My eyes fall to the bruises and she shifts uncomfortably. "If I was a normal guy, I'd leave it. But seeing those marks on your skin does something to me. What happened?"

"It doesn't matter. It's done with now," she mutters, clearly irritated by my questions.

"If you don't tell me, then I'll make my own version up and it might get blown out of proportion. Maybe it's not as bad as I'm thinking." She remains quiet. "Let me tell you what I'm picturing." I run my finger along her collar bone. Her eyes stare into mine and she licks her lips. She wants me to kiss her. I gently cover each bruise with my fingers until my hand is placed on her neck pretty much how I imagine Reggie gripped her. "I think Reggie grabbed you just like this," I whisper. My mouth is inches away from hers and I feel her breath hitching. "And then, I think he . . . " I slowly run my tongue over her lower lip, and she sucks in a breath. "Tried to kiss you. Did he hurt your lip when you tried to stop him?" She shakes her head. "So that means he bit your lip on purpose?" I ask. Anna doesn't reply.

I gently brush my lips against hers. When she doesn't pull away, I run my free hand into her hair and gently tug her head back. She gasps and it's the opportunity I need to take the kiss deeper. Our lips seal together, and I swipe my tongue against hers. It takes everything in me not to completely overpower this moment and drag her somewhere more private because my entire body is crying out for her. Anna's hands grip my shirt and she pushes up on her tiptoes like she's trying to get closer. My cock strains against my jeans and the second she feels it pushing against her stomach, she freezes. The moment vanishes and we step apart, panting for air. "I'll be on the next visit," I growl. I'm angry for allowing myself to get carried away and kiss her like that, and I'm pissed that Reggie put his hands on her.

"No," she says. "It won't happen again."

"Damn right it won't cos I'll be there."

She chews on her lower lip. "Oh my god, I let you kiss me and you have a girlfriend." Her face is full of regret and worry.

"You mean Bonnie?" I ask. "She's not my girlfriend. She's . . . " I pause. What do I say, my comfort blanket? Instead, I go with, "It's complicated."

"Life is always complicated. I can't get involved with complicated." She looks pained for a second before shaking it off and stepping past me. "Sorry," she mumbles. I stare after her.

"What did you do?" asks Cree after they leave. "I was getting somewhere with her hot friend."

"I made a move and she blew me off," I sigh. "Where's Bonnie?"

Cree laughs and slaps me on the back. "Dust yah self off and carry on. I like it."

I leave the bar soon after Anna and head back to the clubhouse. It's a short walk between the bar and the club. Tiny is waiting for me. "She tried to see Ziggy. I thought she was gonna wake the whole club up. She's crazy." No one is a fan of Michelle, not even the club's prospect.

"Where is she now?" I ask.

"Your room. She said she was getting a shower, so I left her to it."

I go into my bedroom and I'm not surprised to see Michelle lying across the bed naked. I roll my eyes as she smiles seductively. "I've been waiting for you."

"Put your clothes on, Michelle," I sigh. I grab one of my shirts from the floor and throw it at her. "We're past those days, don't ya think."

She jumps up and pushes herself against me. I clench my fists because, despite my feelings of hatred, she's still the mother of my kid and my first love. "You're always there for me," she mutters. "Why did I fuck it all up?"

I take her upper arms and gently move her backwards to put space between us. The door opens and Bonnie walks in. She glances back and forth between us. "You need me or not?" she asks. I shake my head and a look of hurt passes over her face. She closes the door and I lean over to lock it. Michelle takes the opportunity while I'm distracted to rub her hand over my cock, but I close my eyes briefly and then remove her hand.

"Get some sleep. You're a mess," I mutter.

"I just want things to be good again," she cries. "Like before."

"Before you messed it all up, you mean?" I hiss. "I've told you before, stop taking that crap and get well again. I can't have you around here like this."

"If I was clean, you'd have me?" she asks with hope in her voice.

"Yes. I'd have you back with the club where you're safe. I'd let you be around Ziggy." I take her face in my hands and use my thumbs to wipe away her tears. "You could take him to school and the park. You could have it all back if you just got clean."

"And you? Could I have you back?" Giving her false hope would be cruel, so I shake my head.

"Get better for Ziggy. He needs his mum around."

Michelle scoffs. "Your mum would never let me come back here. She'd die before letting me be around for Zigg."

"It's not up to my mum. Get clean." It's not that simple, we both know that. If it was, she'd never have gotten that bad in the first place. She loved me and Ziggy. She just made some bad choices and ended up on a slippery slope— one I didn't spot until it was too late. I place a light kiss on her forehead. "Get some sleep. You'll feel better in the morning."

"Lay with me?" she asks, taking me by the hand and leading me towards the bed.

As I strip down to my shorts, my heart hurts. Being so close to her and yet so far away brings back too many bad memories. We climb under the sheets and she lays her head on my chest. "I'm sorry," she whispers. I wrap my arms around her and close my eyes. At least I know she's safe tonight.

My alarm rings out and I stretch. I reach out and find the space beside me is empty. I sigh heavily. Deep down, I knew Michelle wouldn't stick around, but it still stings. My wallet lies open on the bedside cabinet and I reach for it knowing that she's cleaned me out. There was a good amount in there, and it was stupid of me to leave it around. It would have been too tempting for her to resist.

I spot Bonnie coming out of Trucker's room as I make my way down for breakfast. I do a double-take and she shrugs her shoulders. "What?" she asks. "You think I don't need attention too?" I ignore her. The rules of the club are that any of the club girls are fair game unless a member claims them.

Downstairs, Ziggy is watching cartoons with his aunty Leia. "mum is looking for you. She's screwing about your late-night visitor," Leia warns me with a smirk only younger siblings can seem to pull off. It instantly puts me in a bad mood.

I find my mum in the kitchen. She glares at me. "Really, Finn? You couldn't find a decent girl to bring back here?"

"Wasn't like that, Frankie," I sigh. She hates me using her real name instead of mum just as much as I hate her calling me Finn. "She needed to crash somewhere safe."

"She made her choice!" she hisses. "She left and we picked up the pieces. Now she's in your bed?"

"Not in that way. How the fuck did you know anyway?"

"I caught her dirty ass sneaking out of here at six a.m. She didn't expect to see me. I've never seen a person so terrified," she says smugly. "She doesn't deserve your help, Finn. Stop rescuing her."

"You don't get it, mum. Just leave me to deal with Michelle."

I join Leia and Ziggy to watch cartoons. Leia's smug smirk is still firmly in place.

"I find it hilarious that you are in charge around here yet mum yells at you about the company you keep." She laughs. "Now you know how I feel when you boss me around."

"That's different. You're my sister. I'm supposed to vet your boyfriends. You're only nineteen. If Dad were here, he'd be way worse than me."

"Maybe," she says quietly. We all miss him.

I spot Bonnie tidying around the other couches. I go over to her with the intention of apologizing about last night. I don't owe her anything, we've only ever kissed and shared my bed, but I feel bad. "You okay?" I ask.

"Of course," she says flatly. "Why wouldn't I be?"

"Last night wasn't what it looked like. I didn't have sex with Michelle. She needed a place to crash and—"

"Why are you explaining yourself? You don't need to. It's your business. You looked pretty cosy with the green-eyed girl in the bar last night. I expected to see her in your bed." She swipes her cloth over the coffee table and then sighs. "Is it me?" she asks in a low voice. "I've been coming to your bed for weeks, but nothing ever happens. I need to know if it's me."

I shake my head. "No. I told you before that I'm not looking for anything right now. Just the company."

"But we don't even speak. We fall asleep. It's a little weird."

"Maybe we should call it a day. I have a lot going on right now and I don't have the time to dedicate getting to know you properly right now. I'm sorry."

She shrugs and straightens the couch up. "Whatever."

Cree stands in my office doorway and signals for me to come over. I'm grateful for the interruption. He closes the door before he begins to speak. "I just got a call from the mayor. There was an incident in the early hours. A kid got shot. They're saying it's gang-related, but he wanted me to ask around. Seems this kid wasn't a gang member, just an innocent teenager on his way home from a party. Happened on our streets, Pres."

I rub my beard. "So, you find out who did it yet?"

"I'm working on it. We have to consider that it might have something to do with Reggie. I think we should pay Marshall a visit."

Marshall runs his empire from a storage unit on a back street just behind the railways. The front of the unit is piled high with antique furnishings that he supplies locally, and it's a good way to clean his money up. Once you get to the back of the unit, there are plastic sheets hanging, and behind those sheets sits Marshall's goldmine. Vans are in and out all day collecting furniture stuffed with bags of cocaine and heroin.

When we arrive, it's unexpected, and by the time I push the plastic sheeting to one side, Marshall is rushing forward to greet us. "Gentlemen." He smiles. "I thought I might get a visit from you today."

"Why'd ya think that?" asks Cree coldly.

"I heard about the kid. Naturally, I'd like to know what happened just like you do, but so far, I'm drawing a blank."

"Come on, Marshall. Don't talk shit. You know everything about these streets. I didn't order it, and if you didn't either, someone is stepping on our toes," I say.

"Like?" asks Marshall. "No one would dare."

"Someone fucking did. That's why there's a kid dead," growls Cree, shoving Marshall back a few steps.

"What did Reggie have to say when you turned down his offer?" I ask.

"If you turned him down," adds Cree.

"He wasn't happy. Said I could make so much more on his side of the tracks. He took it well though. Actually, he asked me if I knew where his wife was staying. Did you know his wife was on this side of the tracks?"

I turn and leave with Cree following. It's clear we won't get anything useful from him.

Once outside, Cree turns to me. "It's him, isn't it? He knows you've been sniffing around Anna."

"He don't know shit," I bite out. "How the hell would he? I've hardly seen her. It's not like we went out on a date."

Cree shakes his head. "I don't know, man, but I've got a bad feeling about this. Maybe we should send her back to her side?"

"Are you fucking crazy? He'll kill her. You want that on your conscience? She's nice and so is her kid. She's on this side, which means she's under our protection. Put a brother on her, but I don't want her to know, so make sure he's discrete."

"You want to take this deeper by protecting her? It'll end badly, Pres." I glare at him until he holds up his hands. "Fine, I'll get on it."

Chapter 7

ANNA

Monday morning comes around fast. I feel like my weekend flew by, but I'm also excited to go back to the garage. I spent my first day on Friday learning the system, so today I feel like it's my real first day of work.

I drop Malia at school and thankfully don't see Riggs. Although our kiss is playing on a loop in my head, my decision to stay away from him is the right one. He'll consume me and his life is just as complicated as my own. He said so himself.

When I arrive at work, Gears is under a car. I shout my hello and head straight for the office. My plan today is to sit and input all the invoices into the computer system. There's a good six months' worth, but I'm ready for the challenge.

I get so lost in work that when Eva arrives with a sandwich so we can have lunch together, I'm shocked at the time. "Guess what," she says, leaning closer. "So, you remember Jamie from Friday night?"

"The guy who tried to lick my face off?" I shudder.

"His nephew was killed over the weekend. Shot in cold blood!"

I stop chewing my sandwich and stare at her wide-eyed. "No fucking way. He didn't stop talking about his nieces and nephews. He must be devastated!"

"Chris told me today. It's so sad, isn't it? He was only a kid. Makes you want to stay home when things like this happen in your hometown."

I nod in agreement. "I feel awful for him. Ask Chris to pass on my condolences."

Once Eva leaves, I make the guys a coffee. I take the tray down to the garage floor and almost stumble when I come face to face with Riggs and Cree.

Riggs' eyes fix on me and his expression fills with annoyance. "What the fuck she doing here?" I feel my face flush crimson with embarrassment. I know men don't always take rejection well, but he looks positively pissed.

"Pres, this is Anna," says Gears. "She's working in the office."

"I know who the fuck she is," snaps Riggs. He moves towards me and lifts my chin to inspect my neck bruises again. It feels like an alpha male thing to do— he doesn't even ask or make it less than obvious. They look worse today because I'm not covered in makeup and they've gone yellow now that they're a few days old. "You didn't tell me you had a new job," he mutters.

"I didn't know I needed to," I say, pulling my chin free from his gentle hold. I move around him and go back into the office.

Riggs follows me. "You didn't think it was important to tell me that you were working in my garage?"

"I didn't know it was your garage. I thought Gears was the boss."

"Everyone treating you good here? Being respectful?" he asks, and I nod. "Good. Have you told Reggie you're working here?"

"Why would I tell him? What's with all the questions?" I shuffle some paperwork. I'm irritated by his presence since he looked so pissed to see me again.

"Don't tell him. He won't like it. Things are getting messy on the streets. When you're out alone, you need to be on high alert."

"You're starting to sound just like him," I mutter. "Whatever happens out there on the streets involving all of your little gangs has nothing to do with me. I'm only Reggie's wife on paper. I'm a normal person, a single mum just trying to move on and earn an *honest* living."

"A kid was shot last night. It happened just a few streets away from where you live. I don't know why it happened or if it's gang-related, but either way, you're a target whether you like it or not."

"Jamie's nephew?" I ask. "The guy I went on a date with, it was his nephew."

Riggs looks troubled. "How'd ya know that?"

"Eva told me just now at lunch. Her date told her and he's friends with Jamie."

Riggs mutters something about having to go and rushes out the office, slamming the door behind him. I stand at the window overlooking the garage and see Riggs talking quietly in Cree's ear, and then they both look up at me. I step away from the window. I don't like the look of worry on Riggs' face, and if it's anything to do with Reggie, then I don't want to know.

When I collect Malia from school, she's excited and bouncy. "Mummy, can I go to Ziggy's house? Pleeeease," she begs.

We're already almost home, so I shake my head, thankful that she waited until now to ask me and not in front of Ziggy's grandma.

"I don't think that's a good idea. Are you playing with other kids like I told you to?" I ask. She shakes her head and her little natural curls bounce. "Malia, you promised to try and make some new friends," I sigh.

"The other kids don't like me," she says. "Ellis said that my daddy is a bad guy. He isn't allowed to play with me. Is daddy bad?"

"What?" I almost screech. "Why didn't you tell me he said that?"

"I'm telling you now," she says, rolling her eyes, and I laugh at her sassiness. "Is my daddy bad?"

I push the key into the lock and open the front door. "Just ignore what people say about your daddy. He loves you and you love him. I think . . . " My words die on my lips as I survey the living room. The place is a mess— things are all over the floor and the mirror is smashed. I swoop down, wrap Malia in my arms, and go back outside. My hand is shaking as I press Eva's name on my mobile phone. "Hey girlfriend," she answers in a high-pitched voice.

"Eva, are you at home?"

"Yeah, what's up?" she asks.

"I've been burgled," I explain. I hear her rustling about, and she tells me she's on her way. Luckily, she lives just at the end of my road, and Esther, her mum, lives a few doors away from Eva. Minutes later, they both come running towards me. "I didn't know what to do," I say feebly. Esther rubs my arm to offer reassurance as she passes me and goes into the house.

The rumble of motorbikes fills the street, and Malia covers her ears. "Have you called the cops?" asks Eva, but I shake my head. "Did you call him?" she adds as Riggs' bike comes to a stop outside my house. I shake my head again.

Riggs steps off his bike followed by Cree and two other bikers. "You okay?" he asks.

"Not really. I've been burgled," I mutter. "What are you doing here?"

"I was passing," he says and then heads inside.

Esther comes back out. "The place is a mess. You can't stay here tonight," she says. "Every room's been ransacked."

Riggs comes out with his mobile phone pressed to his ear. He pushes a bag into my hands. "Pack some shit together. Just stuff for a few days."

Eva and Esther help me get some things together while Malia clings to me. "Who would do something like this?" sighs Eva, looking around my bedroom at the heaps of clothes and other belongings strewn all over the place. "It doesn't even look like they've taken anything."

My jewellery box lays untouched on the dresser. It's full of expensive pieces that Reggie bought me.

Back outside, Riggs is waiting beside his bike. He flicks his cigarette to the ground and crushes it with his boot. "All packed?" he asks, and I nod in response. "The police are on their way. They won't get any fingerprints and the chances of them finding whoever did this are low. I'm gonna do some digging. Until I know for sure that this isn't targeted, I'm gonna have someone follow you."

"No," I say firmly as I hand Malia to Esther. "Take her for me. I'll be over shortly." I wait until they're gone before fixing Riggs with a hard stare. "I spent years being followed around by Reggie's men. I won't have that again. This wasn't targeted. I was unlucky that some chancer broke into my house—"

"What did they take?" he cuts in. When I don't reply, he smirks. "Exactly. My guy's been watching you. You haven't spotted him once, so he's not gonna be all up in your face." He points over to where a man stands by the wall at the end of my street.

"That's how you knew something was wrong," I gasp. "Why would you have someone follow me?" I ask. I'm outraged that he's taken it upon himself to arrange for me to have protection without my knowledge or consent.

"Because I can." He brushes his thumb over my lower lip. "I've been dreaming about your mouth ever since that kiss," he mutters. His voice is low and raspy. I'm suddenly mesmerized by his lips. "Stop looking at me like that," he whispers. "It makes me do stupid things."

I snap out of the spell when I hear the word stupid. He's right. I step back. "Who's your guy?" I ask, nodding to the shadow at the end of the street.

"Blade. He got the name because he can throw any sized blade accurately. He's been known to hit his target right between the eyes."

"Nice," I mutter. "I don't think that'll be needed, but if it makes you happier." I shrug and walk away.

The week drags. The police came, and as Riggs suggested, there were no prints. I gave my statement, and as nice as it was to stay with Eva, I was glad to get back home a few days later. I pop my head out of the front door and Blade glances up from his cell phone. "You want coffee?" I ask. He smiles gratefully and takes the steps two at a time.

I got sick of seeing him sitting on my wall all the time and told him that if he was going to keep following me around, then he could at least allow me to get to know him.

"Have you heard from Riggs?" I ask casually, because since my place got burgled, I've not heard a thing.

"Yeah, I saw him last night at the club. You hot for the Pres?" he grins.

"No," I say, feeling my cheeks heat up. "He irritates me. He's with that girl, anyway, erm . . . Bonnie?"

Blade grins wider. "You trying to dig for info?"

"No. I already know he's with her. I saw them together when we were out a week or so ago." I hand him his coffee.

"Well, she's in his bed every night, but that doesn't mean shit unless he lays claim to her," he says.

"Lay claim?" I repeat.

"Yeah. A biker usually lays claim to the girl he loves. Then she becomes his ol' lady. Once he's done that, they're official. It's like having a wife. No other brother can take her."

"Sounds very old fashioned. Maybe even a little caveman."

He laughs. "Just the way it is."

"So do you have an ol' lady?"

"No way. I love pussy too much. Who wants to have the same one every day for the rest of their life?" He visibly shudders and I laugh.

"It's Friday night. Surely, you have better places to be than here?" I ask.

"The Pres is on his way to relieve me. Should be here any minute," he says. "Then you can ask him all the questions you like!" He grins.

"What!" I screech. "But I'm staying home. I don't need anyone watching me."

Blade shrugs again. "If the Pres says you need watching, then you need watching. He won't take no for an answer." Blade presses his ringing cell to his ear. "Okay, Pres. I'm inside." He cuts the call and then goes to open my front door.

I watch from the kitchen as Riggs fills the doorway. "Why are you in the house?" he asks Blade suspiciously.

"She asked me in for coffee. We've become like bezzie mates these last couple of days, haven't we, Angel," says Blade, winking at me. Riggs scowls. "I'm free to go then?" asks Blade. Riggs moves to one side to allow Blade to leave. "See you tomorrow. I love bacon with pancakes for breakfast."

I laugh at his hint for me to cook breakfast tomorrow. Riggs slams the door shut with his boot. "Asshole," he utters.

"Riggs, you really don't have to babysit me. Nothing's happened since the break-in."

"Riggs," says Malia, bouncing around his feet and reaching her arms up. I frown at her over-familiar behaviour, but Riggs doesn't seem to mind and he reaches down and picks her up. "Ziggy wants me to come to play at your house," she says, patting his beard with her tiny hand. "Can I?"

"Malia," I hiss. "That's rude."

"It's fine with me if it's fine with your mummy," says Riggs. "In fact, the club's having a party tomorrow. There'll be lots of kids Malia's age. Why don't you both come? You could ask Eva seeing as Cree won't stop asking me about her," he says.

I start to shake my head, because being around Riggs isn't such a good idea. "Please, mummy," whines Malia.

"Or I'm happy to have Malia for a few hours if you don't want to come," says Riggs. "I know you're finding it hard to resist me." He grins playfully. "Let's watch cartoons, Malia, so mummy can make her mind up," he says, taking Malia to sit on the couch.

"How come Blade isn't supposed to come inside the house but you are?" I ask, standing in the doorway.

"Because I gave myself permission," he replies. "I'm in charge, remember?"

"Of your gang," I say cheekily. "But you're not in charge of me. I can have whoever I like around for coffee."

He grins to himself and keeps his eyes on the television as he mutters, "Sure you are, Angel. Sure, you are."

"I haven't heard from you all week," I say and then instantly regret it because I sound needy and bothered.

"That bother you?" he asks, arching a brow in that sexy way of his.

"No, just . . . if you're busy, then you really don't need to be here. Eva's coming over for a drink and to catch-up."

"I'm not busy, Anna."

The front door opens and Eva walks in holding two bottles of wine. She sees Riggs and mouths the words 'What the fuck' to me. I shrug and nod towards the kitchen. "Will you be okay for a minute?" I ask him and he nods. He looks more engrossed in the cartoon than Malia does.

"What the hell is he doing here?" whispers Eva when we get into the kitchen.

"He's on Anna watch tonight. Blade left ten minutes ago."

"You lucky bitch," she grins. "How do I get a gorgeous man like that to watch over me?"

"You know how I feel about all of this," I say. "It's over the top and pointless. Reggie can get to me any time he wants, we both know that." I shake one of the bottles of wine she brought with her. "Let's get this baby open. You pour and I'll put Malia to bed."

Chapter 8

RIGGS

I sigh as Eva leans in closer. She and Anna have drunk far too much wine. "So, Riggs, we were wondering—"

"Erm, no, WE weren't," interrupts Anna. "You were!"

Eva giggles and waves her wine glass dismissively. "I was wondering what special requirements you need to meet to join the Kings Reapers?" she asks.

"What do ya mean?" I ask as I scroll through my mobile phone idly.

"All the men are gorgeous. They all have tattoos. Most have beards. All have muscles," says Eva, counting them off on her fingers. "If a thin, frail fifty-year-old asked to join, would he fit the requirements?"

"First of all," I sigh, placing my phone on the worktop. "There are no requirements. Most of the men in my club have grown up around this life. Some are ex-Forces. Tiny, for example, is ex-forces. No one would just turn up at the club and ask to join. Tiny knew Rock and when he left the Army, he was struggling to cope. You form a band of brothers when you're out there fighting together. To come home to nothing is hard."

"So they come looking for a similar support system?" asks Anna thoughtfully.

"I guess," I shrug. "My grandfather started the club for that reason. He needed to feel that he had brothers to watch his back."

"Are you single?" slurs Eva, seemingly bored of the serious conversation.

"Who wants to know exactly?" I ask, staring at Anna.

"Who was the girl at the club sucking your face?" Eva asks.

"That was Bonnie," Anna says, answering before I can. "*It's complicated*," she adds, rolling her eyes and using her fingers as quote marks.

"Oh, tell us more. We love to solve love dilemmas, don't we, Anna?" says Eva eagerly.

"It's not complicated because we aren't together," I say.

"When I asked you before, you told me it was complicated," Anna says accusingly.

I'd said that to stop conversations like this. I don't want to go into details about why I keep Bonnie around. "I'm telling you we're not together. End of."

"What about Ziggy's mum?" asks Eva, and Anna nudges her hard and scowls. "What?" laughs Eva.

"Stop being nosey," says Anna.

"Now, that is complicated," I say. "And you don't like complicated, do you, Anna? So, there's no point in me telling you." I grab my kutte. "I have shit to do. Are you gonna be okay?" Anna nods. "I'll send someone to get you tomorrow, around two p.m." She stares at me blankly. "For the party. Bring Miss Nosey too," I say, nodding at Eva.

Anna follows me to the door. "Thanks, and I'm sorry about Eva. She believes in love and romance and all that bollocks."

I turn to face her. We're inches apart and I watch the way her tongue runs across her lower lip. "Do you believe in it?" I whisper, but she shakes her head. "Pity," I add, and then I kiss her lightly on the head. It feels like such a natural thing to do that it's only when I step outside that I register the shock on her face.

When I get to The Windsor, Cree is in my pops' corner, so I go to him. "You find anything out?" I ask. He nods and then offers me the bottle of bourbon. I drink straight from the bottle. "Okay, hit me with it."

"It's Reggie for sure. The dead kid, the break-in at Anna's—he knew about that guy and Anna going out on a date, so he took the guy's nephew out."

I give a low whistle. "Fuck. Extreme."

"For sure. He isn't kidding. He wants us to send Anna back to his side of the tracks."

I shake my head, because there's no way that's happening. "What is it with this woman, Riggs? You fucking her?"

"No. Honestly, brother, I don't know what it is, but I'm not sending her back to him. Did you find out when the injunction runs out?"

Cree takes a drink from the bottle and hands it back to me. "Yep. You ain't gonna like it. The judge granted it for three months. Long enough for Anna to find somewhere else to live. It runs out next month. After then, he can turn up at her house and she can't stop him. It also means the visiting with his kid at the safe centre will come to an end. Do you think she knows all this?"

I rub my beard and sigh. "I don't know, brother. The only thing saving her at the minute is the banning order and the fact she's this side of the tracks."

"The fact is he's killing on our side without having to step a foot over the tracks. We can't allow that shit to continue.

How far is he gonna go to get her back?" Cree drinks from the bottle. "We gotta decide what to do, brother. If you aren't willing to send her back, then we have to show him we're not gonna take his shit."

"I know. She's coming to the party tomorrow. I'll corner her to see how much she knows about the injunction order. She isn't saying much when it comes to Reggie."

Cree looks brighter. "Is she bringing her hot friend?" I nod and he grins. "My weekend suddenly got a lot better."

It's almost half past two by the time Chains sets off to collect Anna and Malia. Ziggy is pacing by the gate waiting. He was so excited when I told him about his friend coming to play.

Bonnie takes a seat on my lap, making sure to rub her ass against me. We've come to an understanding— she can fuck who she likes, but she spends the night in my bed. She rests back against me lazily.

Ziggy jumps up on the gate as it opens and then he runs after Chains' truck. I smile at his excitement when he sets his eyes on Malia. The kid really loves her. I move Bonnie from my lap and make my way over to where Anna and Eva are. "Ladies," I greet. I kiss Anna on the head and she smiles shyly. "Drinks are in the bathtub over there." I point to the overflowing old tin bath which Lake is topping up with ice. "Food is cooking on the grill and Gears will give the shout when it's ready. The kids can't get out of here, the fence is all the way around, so we usually let them run wild."

Anna smiles as Ziggy and Malia run past us towards the bouncy castle. Cree saunters over holding two bottles of beer. He hands the girls one each and winks at Eva. She blushes and I decide it's the perfect time to whisk Anna off for a chat. "Follow me," I say, gently taking her hand. I lead her to an empty picnic blanket, and she takes a seat.

"There're so many people here," she says, looking around.

"Yeah, these parties are popular and our other charters usually come up for the weekend."

"Charters?" she repeats. I forget she doesn't know this life.

"Our club is spread over different counties. All of us are the Kings Reapers, but I run the London Charter, Gunner over there runs the Nottingham charter, and so on. We're a big club."

"Wow, who knew there were so many people that loved bikes."

I smile and lean back on my hands. "Visiting day for Malia tomorrow?"

Anna looks sad for a moment. "At the contact centre this time, though," she clarifies. "He can't do anything there."

"Is that a permanent thing?" I ask. "Or will he eventually be able to see her outside of there?"

Anna drinks some of her beer. "Do you stay with Ziggy when he visits his mum?"

I scoff. "He doesn't let me leave. The kid clings to my neck so tight, he practically chokes me."

"That's sad that he doesn't feel safe to stay with her. I'd hate that if Malia wouldn't stay with me."

"He's traumatised from living with her before he came to me. When she first gave birth to him, we tried to make it work. It was good for the first year and then she got into a bad crowd." I take a deep breath. I hate talking about this shit, but with her it feels good to explain. "She left me, took my kid and ran. I didn't see either of them for a year. When I found her, she was living in a run-down house with her so-called friends coming and going whenever they pleased. Ziggy was pale from never going outside. She didn't feed him properly, so he was too thin." I shake my head. The memory of the first time I saw Ziggy after I found them breaks my heart. "I don't know what happened to him in the year he was with her, but he was a nervous wreck. I applied for custody and she didn't fight it. I've had him ever since."

Anna gives me a sympathetic smile. "That's so brave of you. Not many men would stand up and do that. He's doing so well now, you wouldn't know any of that happened by looking at him," she says.

"I can't take all the credit. My mum, Frankie," I point to where she's sitting, "and my sister, Leia, help me a lot. I'm lucky to live here with the Kings because we're one big family and we all take care of each other's kids. It's a free for all in there," I smirk. "Ziggy loves it."

"Sounds amazing." That sad look passes over her face again. "I don't see my family all that much."

"No?"

She shakes her head. "I grew up in care, so hearing Ziggy's story touches me. I wish I'd had a dad like you to save me."

"You don't know your parents?" I ask.

"I know my mum. I went into care when I was three, but I still saw my mum for visits every few months. I was allowed to go back to her when I turned fifteen, but by then I was on a slippery slope to nowhere good."

"All teenagers go off the rails," I reason, and she gives a snort. "So, you got in with a wrong crowd?"

"I guess. My mum wasn't one for rules, so I was free to come and go as I pleased. By seventeen, I was out drinking and hanging out in bars. That's how I met Reggie."

"You were seventeen?" I ask. Reggie must have three or so years on me, which makes him at least six or seven years older than Anna.

She nods. "Almost eighteen. He was twenty-four. I was pregnant and married within months. I didn't have time to think it through."

We fall silent and I process what she's told me. Reggie would have moulded her into exactly what he wanted. I'm conscious of the fact he could still hold some power over her. "Do you know the judge only gave you a short-term injunction? Reggie can have full visiting rights from next month on."

Anna chews on her lower lip. She almost looks vulnerable. "Yeah. It's all Reggie would agree to. I took whatever I could get."

"What was the point?" I ask.

"It gave me enough time to get away from him. We've separated a lot over the years. Usually, I find a place and he allows that space for a while, but then he makes me go home. It's like he humours me— he calls it my tantrums. But this time, because of how serious it was when he hurt me, I decided to push for the injunction to give me time. A new female cop had joined the force and she wanted to do things by the book. She stood up for me all the way. She was amazing. She suggested I come here, where he couldn't get to me so easily."

"So, you came here, got the space you needed, but now what?"

Anna begins to chew on her thumb nail. "I don't know. I'm done running. I guess it's something I've always done. I know he knows where I am. I know he can come anytime he wants, but we seem to play this game of cat and mouse. I feel like I should do things differently this time so that he knows I'm serious."

"And moving over the tracks was your solution?"

"I know he can still get to me. He can use other people. But so far, he's left me alone. I know it won't continue, but the peace has been nice. It's only been a short time, but I feel like it's different this time. He can't just turn up here and drag me home like he's done before." She smiles sadly and I want to be the one who makes her smile again. "I think he agreed to the three-month banning order to give me thinking time. I think that he thinks I love him and I'll go back to him."

"Do you love him?" I hold my breath waiting for her answer.

"No. I did, but I don't anymore." She uncurls her legs from under her and straightens them out. I brush my finger over her foot and her skin breaks out in bumps.

"He didn't deserve your love," I say quietly. I gently slide her foot out of her sandal and place it in my lap, then reach for the other and do the same. "You deserve a man who can treat you like a queen," I add, rubbing her foot between my thumb and fingers. She groans and closes her eyes, leaning back on her hands. I admire the way her cheeks turn pink and the flush spreads down her neck. I desperately want to see all of her, to see how far that blush goes.

Eva and Cree come over and hand out shot glasses. They take a seat on the blanket and top up each glass with a clear liquid. "You two looked sad as fuck. We thought we'd cheer you up," says Cree. The spell is broken, and Anna pulls her feet from my lap and crosses her legs. We clink glasses and drink. I wince as the liquid slips down my throat, burning as it goes.

After a few more drinks, Anna relaxes. She throws her head back and laughs at something my mum says to her. There's a feeling building in my chest and whenever I look at Anna, it gets stronger. I've not felt it since Michelle and I'm not sure if I'm strong enough to ignore it.

"Pres, am I in your bed tonight?" asks Bonnie, sidling up to me on the blanket. I feel Anna glance briefly in our direction, but with Cree and Eva talking and my mum and Leia, I'm certain she didn't hear.

"I'll let you know," I mutter quietly.

"It's just I'm horny as fuck and I need—" I cut her off before she can finish her sentence.

"Enough," I growl. She presses her lips together and moves away from me.

Anna pushes up from the ground. "Toilet?" she asks, and I point towards the clubhouse.

"Straight through to the back. The red door." I wait for her to leave and then I turn to my mum. "She's nice, right?"

"Really nice. Her kid's sweet too. You wouldn't think she was Reggie's kid."

"You wouldn't think she'd spent years with Reggie either. She's so innocent to this kind of life. If he did anything right, it was that he shielded her from it all," I say. "Can you keep an eye on Ziggy and Malia? I need to talk to Anna alone." mum gives me a knowing smile and I head inside after Anna.

I meet her as she comes out of the bathroom. She looks up in surprise as my hands brush each of her cheeks gently. Her chest rises and falls and her tongue darts over her lips again. I move my mouth inches away from hers and she sucks in a breath. I smile right before I press my lips against hers. I kiss her with everything I have. I pour my soul into her because it's all I've thought about since the second she sat on the blanket next to me today. Hell, it's all I've thought about since she walked into The Windsor with her bad attitude. I back her to the wall until she's cornered.

When I pull back, she glares at me. "What the fuck was that?" she hisses. "I heard you and Bonnie less than five minutes ago."

"It's not what you think," I begin.

"It never is with men like you," she huffs. "It sounded pretty much like you were keeping her on hold in case you got lucky with me!"

"Fuck, that's not what that was," I groan. "I haven't had—" I stop talking when Rock passes on his way to the bathroom. "Shit," I grumble.

I take Anna by the hand and pull her towards my office. She tries to get free, but I turn to her, my patience wearing thin. "Stop!" I warn and she glowers at me.

"Make me," she hisses. I swoop down and throw her over my shoulder. "Riggs!" she yells, hitting my lower back with her small fists. I grin because she's no idea how her fighting turns me the fuck on.

Once we step inside the office, I place her down. "I've never had sex with Bonnie. She stays in my bed, but we don't do anything like that." Anna stares at me sceptically. "I don't sleep," I confess. I tap the side of my head. "It's always fucking busy in here. I know it sounds fucked up, but the only time I can sleep for more than an hour at a time is if someone's sleeping next to me."

"Like a comfort blanket?" she mutters.

"Maybe," I shrug. "Who fucking knows? I just know it works, and if I don't sleep, then this place goes to shit. I'm crazy when I'm tired." It's the most I've ever told someone I hardly know, especially a woman. Even Bonnie's never had a full explanation. I rake my fingers over my head. "It sounds stupid, but it's the truth. Bonnie and I aren't fucking."

Chapter 9

ANNA

I throw myself at Riggs. It's my body's automatic reaction to him and the confession he just gave me. I'm tired of suppressing how I really feel and the shots of alcohol that Eva plied me with have helped loosen me up.

He catches me with a surprised look on his face. I wrap my legs around his waist and press my lips to his. This seems to kickstart him into action and he holds me tight against him. We kiss and nip at each other hungrily. His hands squeeze my ass and I can feel his erection through his jeans. I grind against him, unashamed because I need him. It's been a long time since I've felt attractive or wanted, but he makes me feel both of those things with just one smouldering look.

We crash against the office wall and the pictures shake from the impact. "Lose the shirt," he growls. I waste no time pulling it over my head and dropping it to the floor.

He kisses me hungrily. His mouth works down my neck and chest until he's tugging the cup of my lace bra down. He nips the soft plump flesh and flicks his tongue over my erect nipple. I hiss, throwing my head back and arching my back from the wall. The feel of his beard against my skin is causing reactions way down deep and soaking my panties. I begin rubbing myself against him again, needing to feel friction *there*.

He lowers me to my feet and towers over me with his hands at either side of my head. "Lose the bra," he demands. I reach around the back and unclip it. It falls to the floor as his mouth goes to my other breast. His kisses work down my body until he's on his knees before me. He tugs my shorts down my legs and groans when he comes face to face with my soaked panties. His kisses against my inner thigh become rougher, his beard grazing the sensitive skin there.

He gently lifts my leg and places it over his shoulder. I look down, watching as he moves my panties to one side. I'm torn between needing to feel his mouth on me and wanting to hide. I feel so exposed yet so sexy all at the same time.

He doesn't give me a chance to reconsider or stop him. His tongue sweeps up the length of my pussy in a swift motion that causes me to jerk. It's so sensitive that I almost climax right away.

"Fuck, you taste good. If you are the last thing I taste before I die, I'll die happy," he mutters. He repeats the motion again like he's leisurely licking an ice cream. I cry out and my legs almost buckle from underneath me. He runs a finger over my opening and slowly pushes it inside of me. "You ready, Angel?" he asks. I run my fingers over his head. I want him back there, but at the same time, I want to push him away. I feel like jelly and I can't form the words, so I stare down at him lazily and nod my head. He smirks. "Keep your eyes on me. It's sexy as fuck," he growls. He presses his mouth against my pussy and begins a punishing and relentless act of licking, sucking, and nipping. I'm so close to the edge that tears leak from the corners of my eyes and my head falls back against the wall.

Riggs nips my inner thigh. "Eyes, Anna!" he growls in warning and I bring my head back to watch him. He circles his thumb over the swollen bud and smirks when I cry out again.

A warmth burns through my body and I shudder hard. I grip his head to steady myself as an intense orgasm rips me apart. I shake and shudder uncontrollably. It's something I've never experienced before, and when I look back at Riggs, I feel so exposed that I drop my leg back to the ground and instantly cover myself with my hands. He rises to his feet with a satisfied smile on his face. He uses his thumbs to wipe the tears from my eyes and then licks the salty water from each. "We need to get back out there."

Panic and guilt hit me hard. "Fuck," I hiss, grabbing my shorts. "I left Malia."

"She's fine." He smiles, looking relaxed. "My mum is watching her and Ziggy. Plus, Eva's there."

"That's not the point. I left my child with a bunch of strangers while I let you . . . well, you know," I mutter as I pull my clothes back on. "I don't usually do that," I mutter, feeling like he needs to know I'm not the kind of girl to hook up with strangers.

He catches my hand before I can rush off and moves in close, invading my space again. "Don't do that. Don't push me away like what we just shared wasn't fucking hot. If that's how hard you come from just my mouth, imagine what it'll be like when I fuck you," he whispers close to my ear. "You're not the type of girl to fuck around, I hear that. But now I've had a taste of you, I won't be letting you go easily."

He takes me by the hand and leads me back outside. Everyone is exactly how they were when we went, laughing and chatting. Meanwhile, my legs are threatening to give way from his alpha threat. I should be alarmed, but I'm weak for a bossy ass and Riggs only needs to look at me to make me want to rip off my clothes and lay myself out for him. I give my head a shake. *What the fuck is wrong with me?*

Malia is still exactly where I left her— sitting on the picnic blanket next to Ziggy, eating a burger. My heart swells with love around the same time that mum guilt kicks in. Do I really want another man in my life after everything I've already been through? He has the ability to distract me so much that I neglected her for a short time.

Eva eyes where our hands are joined and arches her brow. I pull my hand free and Riggs gives me a quizzical stare. "You let me eat your pussy, but you don't wanna hold my hand?" he asks.

"Shh," I hiss. "Things got a little out of hand back there," I mutter. "Maybe we—"

Riggs shakes his head in disbelief. "No!" he snaps. "You're not doing that. Fuck, Anna." He mutters, "You're gonna make me lose my mind with this hot and cold bullshit." He shakes his head and mutters something as he storms away from me.

I drop down next to Eva and bury my face in my hands. "Man trouble?" she asks with a laugh.

"For a change," I say sarcastically.

"I wouldn't mind if Riggs was the reason for my man trouble," she grins, wiggling her eyebrows.

"I hear you have your own hot admirer." I smirk and when she looks at me blankly, I add, "Cree?"

"What?" She laughs. "He hardly spoke two words to me. He seems a bit moody for me."

"Um, brooding hot man," I say, wiggling my eyebrows back at her, and she giggles. "Maybe he's just shy around girls," I suggest.

Eva scoffs. "Have you seen the size of him? He puts the Hulk to shame. Guys like that know women well. I can't imagine he's shy or scared to talk to women. I think he just dislikes me . . . a lot. Anywho, stop changing the subject from you and Riggs. What happened?"

I feel myself blushing and Eva gasps like she's just added two and two together and came up with five. "No," I mutter. "We didn't have sex," I clarify, and she looks disappointed. "It doesn't even matter because nothing can happen between us."

"Why?" she asks.

"Umm, let me think," I say sarcastically while tapping my chin. "My psycho ex for a start. Then there's the fact he lets a girl who he's not actually in a relationship with share his bed every night, and he tells me it's complicated. He's in a gang. He's got a messed-up ex too. The list goes on."

"He's good looking. He's big and scary so he might manage to get rid of your psycho ex. He's got a smouldering sexy look about him. He's got to be great in bed. I bet he has a huge cock. He produces cute kids," she counters, and I laugh and shove her gently.

I groan. "My head is telling me it's not a good idea to pursue him."

"And what's your heart telling you?" she asks.

"Last time I listened to that, I ended up in a bad way," I mutter.

"So, you're gonna spend the rest of your life alone? Do you think Reggie's alone? He would have had someone else in your half of his bed the same day you packed your bags. Not every man will treat you like shit, Anna."

I watch Riggs talking to his mum. His hands are in his pockets and he's digging his boots into the dusty ground. Even with a sullen look, he's hot. Ziggy taps him on the leg and his face lights up. He picks his son up and his sexiness level triples. "Shit, how hot is he with his kid in his arms," groans Eva, and I nod in agreement. "Just imagine having your own little Malia/Ziggy look-alike. You guys would have the cutest kids," she coos, and I roll my eyes again.

"Stop with that kind of talk. It'll never happen."

An hour later, Malia snuggles up against me. "I think she's tired," I say, and Eva pulls out her mobile to call us a cab.

The cab arrives ten minutes later. I look over to see Riggs laughing with Bonnie. She's on his lap again, and even though he's told me there's nothing sexual between them, I can't stop the feeling of jealousy that drips through me when I see them looking so intimate. If I decided to let him into my life, would he stop sharing his bed with her, or would he still need her to be his comfort? It's those kinds of questions that hold me back. We leave without saying goodbye.

I get home and bathe Malia and settle her into bed. She's exhausted after her afternoon with Ziggy. I slip into some shorts and a vest, and I'm about to choose a film to watch when there's a knock at my front door. I check the time. It's almost eight, so I cautiously check through the spyhole first. I'm surprised to see Riggs waiting patiently. I open the door and he takes my face in his hands and kisses me hard. "You didn't say goodbye," he mutters against my lips.

"You were busy," I say.

He presses another kiss to my lips and then turns and jumps down the steps. "Goodnight, Anna." I watch as he jogs away down the street and as I close the door, I can't stop the smile playing on my lips.

The following day, Malia skips happily by my side towards the contact centre. She looks forward to coming here because she gets to play in a room full of toys with her dad. I shielded her well from all of the negativity surrounding me and Reggie, and even when he would whisper threats in my ear, she'd remain unaware because I would always smile and act like everything was fine.

"Riggs," Malia suddenly screeches excitedly and breaks free from my grip on her hand. I watch confused as Riggs picks her up and spins her around.

"What are you doing here?" I ask. I'm horrified to see him here knowing that Reggie could arrive at any moment.

"I came to support you," he shrugs.

"No, you can't be here, Riggs. I mean it," I hiss. "By being here, you're putting me and Malia in danger."

"You'll never be in any danger again. Not now that you have me in your life," he says casually.

"What does that even mean?" I growl. I glance around to make sure Reggie hasn't arrived. "Seriously, you need to leave."

"Reggie's starting a war with the Kings," he says. "It won't be long before he knows about us."

"Us?" I cry. "What are you talking about?" I feel hysteria coming on. I take Malia from him because seeing them together would send Reggie over the edge. Tears fill my eyes. "Please, Riggs. I'm begging you. Don't bring me into your war."

"He's starting it because of you," says Riggs firmly. "That kid, it was no coincidence that it was Jamie's nephew and you just happened to go on a date with him." My breathing becomes shallow and bile lingers in the back of my throat. I wipe my mouth and realize my hand is shaking. It has to be a coincidence. I can't be the reason that Jamie's nephew is dead. "Reggie wants you home, Anna," says Riggs. "But newsflash, you're mine now and nobody can take what's mine."

I glare at him. "I'm not a piece of furniture for you and Reggie to own. I'm a person and I make my own decisions."

He moves to my ear so Malia can't hear. "Don't tell me you don't want me to own you, Anna. I felt you come on my tongue. We could have that every day."

A black car with darkened windows rolls to a stop and I feel faint. I watch as Reggie steps out of the car and surveys the scene before him. A slow smile forms on his face. It reminds me of the look he'd give me before laying into me. "Aww, the lovebirds are waiting to greet me."

"Reggie Miller. Long time since I saw you. You're not aging well," says Riggs casually.

"Finn 'Riggs' James. A pleasure as always," replies Reggie dryly.

Malia reaches for her dad and he takes her from me. I try to reign in the anxiety that I'm feeling right now. There's nothing to stop Reggie from shooting me and Riggs right here in the street and taking Malia with him. "As lovely as the reunion is, I only have an hour to spend with my daughter." He passes by us and heads inside with Malia.

I turn to Riggs. "Go. I'll call you later."

"He's seen me now. You heard him say lovebirds. He already knew about us before we did. Stop looking so worried." He shakes his head and leads me inside.

Riggs sits next to me as I take my usual seat outside of the room where Reggie and Malia always go. There's a social worker who stays in the room with them. "He was responsible for the break-in at your house too," he says.

"Don't you think I fucking know that?" I growl. "Do you think I'm stupid?"

"You need to stop burying your head in the sand. Ignoring the problem doesn't make it go away. You have to face it head-on."

"And how do you suppose I do that?" I hiss. "You think I should stand up to Reggie? He's at the top of the chain, just like you. He has so many people willing to do his dirty work. They'd do anything he asked them to. My time is running out and he's stepping up the intimidation. I can't escape him."

"So what the fuck has this all been for? Why did you go to court and get the order out on him if you were just gonna give up? I don't want you to stand up to Reggie on your own. I'm here to help you."

"Fuck," I laugh sarcastically. "You've no idea. He won't stop until I'm dead. That's his end goal. But before that day comes, he takes great pleasure in torturing me— chasing me down, mentally battering me, and physically draining me."

"And you want to carry on like that until he kills you?" snaps Riggs.

"Before you got involved, I was doing okay. He left me alone. Now you've trampled into my life and thrown everything into chaos."

"Let me remind you who put you on my radar! It was you who came into my bar. Fuck, you don't think I've wanted to wipe you from my mind and get on with my life? Because trust me, darlin', it was a lot less complicated before you came along. Cree wanted me to send you back to Reggie's side of the tracks, and honestly, I thought about it." He pauses and rubs his beard. "I'm gonna level with ya— I like you. I didn't set out to, but then shit happens. I tasted your pussy yesterday and now it's like I can't leave you the fuck alone. But if you don't want me near you like that, then that's your choice, but it'd be a damn shame cos we got some fire going on between us. But whatever happens, you're on my side of the tracks. My club will protect you against Reggie and that's not your choice, Angel."

We spend the rest of the visit in silence. I go over his words in my mind. I underestimated how far Riggs would go to let Reggie know what was going on. Then I think of Jamie and my heart hurts. He was so proud of his nephew and because of me, he's lost him. What if Reggie takes someone that Riggs loves? I couldn't live with myself.

When Reggie finally steps out of the room, he waits by the door for me to go to him. He doesn't need any words because I know that warning look in his eyes. Malia will be another five minutes because the social worker always talks to her after a visit to check she's okay.

"I'll be right back," I mutter. Riggs doesn't reply. He's letting me make my own choices and I gently squeeze his hand before going to Reggie.

"Sit," he orders, and we go to the next set of chairs so we're away from Riggs.

"Did you have Jamie's nephew killed?" I whisper.

"If you think I won't put a bullet in your fucking boyfriend because we're here, you're mistaken," Reggie begins. "You went on a date last week and now you're fucking a biker? Christ, Anna, your standards shock me. Is that why you wanted this break? To whore your ass around?"

"He was an innocent kid." I begin to cry. "Why would you do that?"

"I've been patient. I've played your game and through everything, the courts, the police interviews, I've respected that you needed space. Now I see that you've taken our break apart as a chance to fuck anything that shows you a scrap of attention. Your time is up." He turns to me and I'm aware that it's so he can block my view of Riggs. "Do you really think the judge was on your side? I play golf with him every week. I've been in control of this from the beginning." He grips my chin between his index finger and thumb and squeezes. "You were silly to get distracted by him. So, your choices are . . . come home or I'm gonna start picking off people one by one. Everyone you care about. Everyone you love. Our little break ends in less than a month. That's how long you have to get back to where you belong. You fuck the biker and I'll kill him first while you watch." He stands gracefully, a look of calm on his face, and fastens the buttons on his designer jacket. He smirks at Riggs. "You're not a very good guard dog. I could have slit her throat and you let her come to me."

Riggs laughs and nods to where his hand rests in his jacket pocket. "You think I didn't have a gun on you the whole time? That's the last time you speak to her alone, so say your goodbyes. There's a war going on, Reggie, and I'm gonna win it."

"I'll enjoy killing your sister. She's first on my list," grins Reggie. "A virgin, from what I hear. I'll film every man who fucks her before I slit her throat and send her back to you in pieces."

"STOP!" I yell, standing between the two. "Just stop."

"I've already taken what you love, Reggie. I'm already winning," grins Riggs and I glare at him. *Am I just a game? A way to piss off Reggie?*

Malia bounds out of the room, unaware of the tension. She reaches up to Reggie and he kisses her on the head before handing her to me. He then leans in and kisses me on the cheek. "Tick-tock, baby. Time is running out," he whispers, and then he's gone.

Chapter 10

RIGGS

We drive back to Anna's in silence. Malia chatters away to her doll in the back of my car. She doesn't have a clue about all the hostility and danger surrounding her. I come to a stop and Anna gets out, slamming the car door, and then gets Malia from the car seat and slams that door too. I grip the steering wheel and take a deep breath.

Inside, Anna continues to stomp about. Malia goes out into the garden to play on her trampoline. I stand awkwardly in the kitchen, watching Anna wash dishes. I wince each time she slams a plate onto the drainer, surprised that it doesn't shatter. "I'm gonna need to put the club on lockdown," I eventually say.

"I don't know what that means, Riggs. I don't understand your world!"

"It means that we keep all the families safe at the club for a while. Until we have a solution to Reggie's threats. No one can go out and no one can come in without my approval."

"Wow, power trip," she mutters. "Off ya go then. Lock down your little club."

I bite my inner cheek, trying to keep myself calm. I'm getting tired of her attitude and her digs at my club. "You're not getting me, darlin'," I growl. "That includes you."

Anna drops the plate she's washing into the sink and then grips the worktop. I watch the water run from her hands and down the cupboard door. "No. That's not happening."

"Anna, don't be—" I begin.

"No. I want you to leave. Take your guard dog from outside my house too."

I stare at her as she goes back to the dishes. "What if he comes for you?"

"Then I'll deal with it like I always have."

"You're being selfish," I mutter, and she turns to me with outrage. "He's threatened everyone around you. He's already killed somebody. He won't stop until you go back to him," I shout.

"You're wrong. He was fine until I dated. I just won't date. I'll go and talk to him." She hangs her head and bursts into tears. I fold my arms across my chest to stop myself from going to her. It's against everything in me, but I watch silently while she cries.

"You're kidding yourself. He'll punish you by hurting those you love. I'm offering you protection. I'm not asking for you to share my bed or to be my ol' lady. You won't owe me anything. I just want to help you."

"I don't need help. Before you came along, I was doing fine. You turning up today was your way of showing off to Reggie. Using me to wave the red flag and begin your stupid fucking war. I saw the glee in your eyes when you told him you'd won by taking what he loved. I'm not a damn trophy to be used against each other."

Anger rips through me. "That's not what I was doing," I growl, getting in her face. "I came to support you. Reggie already knew about us and you're kidding yourself if you think that he didn't. He watches you, he tracks your movements, and he knows who you see and who you fuck before you even do. I went today to show him that I was behind you one hundred percent. I wanted him to see that I'm not scared and that I'll be there with you. You said you wanted to do this differently from all the times you left him before. This is different. This is a clear message that you are done with him."

"Just go," she cries. "Get out. Look after your club. I'll be fine here."

"What's your next big plan, Anna? Move house again? Rip Malia away from her friends, her school, people who could become closer to you both? I can help you. I can free you from Reggie forever. Let me help," I plead.

Anna's Mobile rings and we both glance at the screen as it vibrates across the worktop. It's Eva. "Hi," mutters Anna, turning away from me slightly. She listens for a minute before gasping. "Right, well, Riggs is here with his car. We can come and get you." She waits again and then sighs. "Okay, I'll set up the spare room." She disconnects the call and then looks at me with her eyes full of worry. "Eva was mugged on her way home from work," she mutters. "Cree is with her at the hospital. He's bringing her here."

"And so it fucking begins," I growl and storm out of the house. I need air and a cigarette, so I wait out front for Cree to arrive.

Cree rushes around to the passenger side and opens the door. He takes Eva by the hand and she slowly gets out of the car. I hiss at the sight of her. She looks like she got in a fight with a boxer. Cree's face is filled with fury, and as I follow them up the path to Anna's house, he looks back at me with an expression that screams murder. Anna meets us at the door and bursts into tears. She takes Eva from Cree and leads her over to the couch. "Outside," mutters Cree and I follow him back out. "Did you see that bastard today?"

I nod. "Yeah. A few threats were thrown. He told Anna he'd be picking everyone off until she goes back to him."

"Right, so we're going on lockdown right away?" he asks.

"Yeah. Anna doesn't want to. She's gonna stay here or run maybe." I shrug. "I don't really know, but either way, she doesn't want to come to the club."

Cree glares at me and the vein in his forehead pulsates with anger. "Are you shitting me? This war started because of her." He growls and then storms back into the house.

"Oh, shit," I mumble, hot on his tail.

Anna looks up when the front door smacks back with force and hits the wall. "Pack your shit up. We're leaving in ten minutes," he orders.

"To go where?" asks Anna.

"Somewhere safe. Move."

"I'm not going to the club. I've already told Ri—" she begins but is interrupted as Cree grabs her upper arm and hauls her towards the stairs.

I sigh. "Come on, man, don't do that," I mutter in a warning tone. I don't like the way he's holding her.

"You realize this is all your fault?" Cree hisses at Anna. "You came into our bar and that made us a target. We don't have a choice but to go to war with your fucking husband thanks to you because stepping down would make us look weak. You should have stayed on your own side of the tracks. But now you're here, we have to protect you." He pulls her to where Eva is sitting. "Look at her. This is what will keep happening if you ignore it. Now, get your shit together and come with us to the club or I will personally dump your ass back where it belongs." Cree turns to me. "I'm taking Eva to get some things and collect her mum. I'll see you *both* back at the club."

Eva takes Anna by the hand. "They can help you. For once in your life, accept the help."

Lockdown is not received well, the least happy being Leia. I show Anna and Malia to their room while Leia is on my ass bitching about college. "Why exactly is this guy a threat to us anyway? We came to an arrangement with him years ago. It's been peace ever since," she whines.

Anna's guilty expression tugs at my heart. "Fuck, Leia. Get out of my face. We're on lockdown. End fucking of."

"I think it's bullshit. If dad was here, he'd—"

"He'd put us on lockdown. Go and help mum with the food," I yell. She practically stamps her feet before stomping away. "Sorry about her," I say. Anna smiles weakly. "She wants to become a nurse. She loves college."

"Can I sleep with Ziggy tonight?" asks Malia. "Like a sleep-over?"

I lift her up into my arms. "Ziggy's room is right across from you and your mummy. Maybe you can lay together for a bedtime story and then go back to your own bed?" I walk across the landing to show her Ziggy's bedroom. His toys are strewn across his floor and his bed is unmade. On this landing, there are only four bedrooms— Mine, Ziggy's, and my mum's, and then the spare room that Anna and Malia will sleep in. Plus, a bathroom at the end of the corridor.

Malia fidgets to get down, so I place her in Ziggy's room and she immediately goes to his toys. I stand in the doorway to Anna's room while she sorts through her bags looking for something. "I don't know why you're fighting this," I eventually say. She stills but keeps her back to me. "I can take on Reggie. I can help if you just do what I say."

"I'm sick of men telling me what to do," she mutters.

"Anna," I groan. "I'm not bossing you around. I'm trying to help. I know how to keep you safe from him. Running away won't work forever. He always takes you back. Listen to me. Let me help."

I leave Anna to think about that and I go in search of Eva and her mum. Eva was pretty bruised up, but she seems to always have this light about her that allows her to see the good in things. Back at Anna's, she joked about needing a new purse anyway. I can see why Cree is drawn to her— she can be the light in his eternal darkness.

Cree wanted them on the same floor as him, and I find them standing by Cree's bedroom door in what looks like a private discussion. Eva nods her head as Cree mutters into her ear. He struggles to talk to girls that he likes. It's not something many people know, maybe just me and Chains, but even back in our Army days, he hated talking to women he took a fancy to. Looking at his well-built, tatted-up frame, you wouldn't believe it, so most girls just think he's being rude.

"I just came to check you were settling okay," I say.

Cree keeps his face close to Eva. He's pissed I've interrupted. Eva smiles politely and nods. "Thanks, Riggs. I really appreciate you taking us all in like this. Anna will too, she doesn't know how to accept help."

"I'll keep working on her," I say.

It's early evening and I'm sitting at the bar when Chains joins me. We have one in the club but usually prefer to go to The Windsor. As that's not possible right now, we have to make do with bottled beer. "I love it when we're all together, but man, this place is busy. I think I'll be spending a lot of time in my room."

"Yeah," I agree. "I don't realize how many of us are out there until we go on lockdown. Leia is pissed. I haven't seen her all afternoon," I say.

"Neither have I," he says quickly. "I don't know where she is." I frown. His behaviour only confirms my suspicions that he's got a thing for her.

Anna enters the room with Eva and my heart skips a beat. Just seeing her makes me happy as fuck even though she's pissed at me right now. "Any plans to claim that?" asks Chains with a smirk.

"Why?" I ask dryly. "If I don't, are you hitting her up?"

"No," he laughs. "But looking as hot as she does in them shorts, I'm guessing it won't be long before one of the brothers does."

I scowl in Anna's direction and she looks over in time to catch it. Her step falters, but I don't have a chance to go over and apologize because Michelle rushes over to me and wraps her arms around my neck. As part of the lockdown, I sent Blade to go and find her and bring her to the club. She's still my responsibility, even if a lot of the guys around here think differently.

"I'm so happy to be here, Riggs. I can spend some real time with Ziggy," she gushes, kissing my cheek. I untangle her from around my neck and see that Anna has turned her back to me. *Great, now I need to explain this too.*

Frankie saunters over, looking pissed. "What's she doing here?" she asks.

"Don't start, mum." I sigh. "You know why she's here."

"Don't you think this will confuse Ziggy?" she asks. "You never could resist her and now she'll be back in your bed!"

"Good to see you too, Frankie," says Michelle as she smiles sarcastically.

"Don't speak to me. If I had my way, you'd be ten feet under the ground right now."

Michelle rolls her eyes. "And don't I know it. You tell me every chance you get. But I'm not, am I? I'm back where I belong."

I see Anna glance over. She can hear every word. "Fuck. Stop the bitch session. mum, she's Ziggy's mother. I can't leave her out there when we're going to war. Please try to be civil for Ziggy's sake. Michelle, you're only here temporarily. It's for your own safety." I turn my back to them all and drink the contents of my beer bottle. "Fucking women," I mutter, wiping my mouth on the back of my hand.

I sink a few more beers before I eventually make my way over to Anna. "Can we talk?" I ask. She doesn't bother to hide the look of annoyance on her face.

We go into my office. "I just wanted to apologize for earlier. When you came down and I was scowling, it was at something Chains said, not at you."

"I have no idea what you're talking about." She sighs.

"And Michelle being here means nothing. I have to keep everyone safe. It's what I do."

"Right. You don't need to explain yourself to me." She folds her arms and stares at the ground.

"But I want to. I want you to know that I'm not what they say."

"What do they say?" she asks.

"I have a reputation to keep. It's the way this life is. But it's important to me that you know it's just a facade. The real me is who I am around you, how respectful I am to you." Her eyes meet mine and I sigh. "I don't want us to be awkward around each other. If you tell me you're not interested, then I get it. I'll back off." I clench my jaw in anticipation of her answer.

"I don't know how I feel, Riggs. I have so much going on right now . . . " she trails off.

I nod in acceptance and add an awkward smile. "That's fine then. I just had to put it out there so we both know where we stand." I shuffle some papers on my desk. "It's all good. Enjoy the rest of your night."

She moves to the door and then hesitates. "I didn't mean—"

"Anna, it's fine. Honestly. Close the door on your way out," I cut in. My pride is dented, and I need some time alone to lick my wounds. She nods and leaves. I flop into my chair and let out a slow breath. It's been a while since I've put myself out there like that. After everything with Michelle, I haven't wanted to.

Cree comes in without knocking. "You okay, Pres?"

I shrug nonchalantly. "You ever regretted saying something out loud cos you know you can't take it back?" I ask. He nods. "Well, that's how I'm feeling right now. I put myself out there and now I feel like an idiot cos the feelings aren't reciprocated. I read it wrong."

"You talkin' 'bout Anna? I'm pretty sure you didn't read it wrong. I've seen the way she watches you."

I shake my head. "No, she told me straight."

"At least you know."

"What happened between you and Eva earlier? It looked pretty intense?"

Cree smirks. "We're not doing that," he says. "We don't do bitch talk. You don't ask me about feelings and shit, and I don't ask you. Now, shut the fuck up."

I laugh. "Fair enough."

Chapter 11

ANNA

I toss and turn in bed. Riggs' words play over in my head. *Why did I play down my feelings? What am I so afraid of?* I sigh. Malia sleeps soundly next to me, but I never sleep well in a new place. Getting out of bed carefully, I go to the bathroom.

On my way back to my bedroom, I hear Riggs' voice and a woman giggling. They're coming up the stairs and I glance quickly around for a place to hide. I'm between the bathroom and my bedroom, and there's nowhere to go because all the rooms on this floor are occupied. I panic. Either way, he'll see me, so I decide to act casual. It's no big deal. *Right.* I'm almost at my door when he stumbles up the last step and laughs. He's quickly followed by Bonnie. She takes his hand to help him up, but he pulls her towards him and tries to kiss her. He misses her mouth and then laughs again. "Come on, Pres, let's get you to bed," says Bonnie.

"Naked. I need skin," he mumbles. He looks up and blinks a few times. "Anna?"

"Anna," Bonnie smiles awkwardly, "I don't suppose you could help me get him to his room?"

I inwardly groan. The last thing I want to do is be close to Riggs when he's about to get naked with Bonnie. "Sure," I shrug.

We each take an arm and struggle to help him stand. He's a big guy, but we eventually manage to guide him to his room. He stares at me the entire time, and I feel so uncomfortable that I'm relieved when we get him into his room. "Thanks, Anna," says Bonnie. "Goodnight."

She follows him into his room and closes the door. I roll my eyes. Riggs' words from earlier today about me seeing the real him come to mind. It didn't seem like he was acting just then. Besides, none of the guys were around to hear him when he said he needed skin, so who was he pretending for?

I go back to bed with images of Bonnie and Riggs naked together and my heart hurts, but at least this confirms that I made the right decision. I have enough problems right now without making things more complicated.

It's been a few days since we came to stay with the Reapers. I'm becoming more settled as the days pass and I can't deny that I love it here. It's the first time I've felt like part of a family. Eva and Esther have always treated me like I belonged with them, but there are so many more people here and everyone is so welcoming. Malia looks so happy that it warms my heart. When we have to leave here, it'll be hard.

Since my midnight encounter with Riggs and Bonnie a few days ago, I haven't seen him. He's around, in his office mainly, but he's avoiding me, and I know it's because I turned him down.

Eva sits down next to me on the couch. Malia is staring at the large screen television in the main room with Ziggy by her side. "These two are so cute," she says, nodding towards the kids.

"She hasn't asked once about school. I thought she'd miss it, but it seems as long as she has Ziggy, she's happy."

"Do you think he's her soul mate?" asks Eva wistfully.

I laugh. "Maybe. I don't believe in all that."

"Anna," she gasps. "You have to believe there is someone out there made for you."

I scoff. "With my luck? No way. My soulmate is probably a drug addict with no teeth and bad body odour."

"Blade, do you believe in soulmates?" Eva asks him as he shovels cereal into his mouth. He pauses and thinks over her question. "No."

She gasps again. "I feel so sad for you both. Please tell me you believe in love at first sight?" she wails. I scoff again and she cries out with mock distress.

"I believe in lust at first sight. I felt it when I met you, Evalyn," Blade grins.

"Umm, I think you feel that with most women you meet, Blade," she says.

"You mean you don't look at me and wonder what's under these clothes?" he asks. "You don't feel the need to rip off my shirt so you can run your hands over—"

"Finish that sentence, I dare you!" growls Cree from the other side of the room.

Blade winks at us and presses his lips together. "Soz, VP. Just kidding."

"Go wash my bike," says Cree without looking up from his laptop.

"Come on," cries Blade. "That's the prospect's job."

"And now it's yours. Get to it." Blade mutters under his breath and stalks out of the club.

"Check out Mr. Jealousy," I whisper to Eva.

"Are you kidding? The most the guy's ever said to me is that I'm not to look at any of his brothers in any way other than as friends. He's odd. He growls at me. He had the chance to kiss me when we first came here, and he didn't. Mixed signals."

"I still think he's shy," I say.

"No, he's not," she scoffs. "I think he's weird. I need a man to tell me straight exactly what he wants. Cree can't put words into a proper sentence."

I raise my eyebrow. "Oh, I don't know about that. He was pretty clear to Blade just then."

"My mum loves him. Says she gets good vibes from his soul," says Eva with a smile.

Leia joins us. I like her, and although there are five years between us, you wouldn't know it. She opens her nursing revision book. "Riggs has paid my tutor to video call me so I can watch the lecture on my laptop," she says. "Can you believe that?" She sounds outraged.

Eva smirks at me. "Gosh, what a beast. How do you put up with him looking out for you like that?" she mocks.

"I know you think I'm ungrateful, but it's not the same. I want to go to college and see my friends."

"Just your friends?" asks Eva, wiggling her eyebrows.

"Trust me, when you have a bunch of over-protective guys who all treat you like their little sister, there are no boys on the scene. If these guys get a whiff of a man, they're like ravaging dogs."

"I think that's sweet," I muse. "I always wanted a big brother to protect me."

"It's not sweet. It's annoying. How am I ever going to lose my virginity?" she whispers, and we laugh. "Nineteen and I live like a fucking nun."

"Leia said a bad word," says Ziggy, and Leia sticks her tongue out at him playfully.

"If I was a boy, it would be totally different. I'd have lost my V-card years back!"

"I hate that it's different for men and women. Equal rights are bull," says Eva. "It's the same argument that men can sleep with as many people as they like and they're heroes, but girls do it and they're hoes. I hate inequality."

"Eva, please. You once turned a guy down because he wanted to go halves on the dinner bill," I groan. "You can't pick and choose when to be equal."

Eva laughs. "He invited me to dinner, he should pay."

"Would you have paid if you invited him?" I ask.

"And that's why I don't invite men to dinner." She laughs again.

"And you once said you wanted to meet a man who would take care of you so you could live the life of a rich woman and shop all day instead of work," I remind her.

"I'd work hard for my man! It would be worth his while to keep me home, where I'd walk around naked so I was always ready to service him." She giggles. "I can't be a working woman during the day and a whore in the bedroom at night. That shit takes it out of you." We all howl with laughter. Cree growls from where he's sitting, his eyes burning into Eva. She grins playfully. "You like that, Cree?" she asks. "The thought of having your woman waiting around for you, naked?"

He gets up from the table and stomps out of the room. Eva laughs harder. "You're so cruel," I whisper. "He's clearly shy."

"Stop saying he's shy." She laughs again. "Look at the size of him. He's just grumpy. Whenever I laugh, he growls. I think I irritate him." I exchange a knowing look with Leia. It's only Eva who doesn't see the way Cree's gaze heats whenever he looks her way.

Esther seems to have become friends with Frankie, and they take the kids off to the kitchen to bake, two proud grandmothers working together.

I take the opportunity to sunbathe around the back of the clubhouse. I borrow a bikini from Leia, and she decides to take a break from studying to join me. "You complain about being here, but I think you're so lucky. I wish Malia had a family like this," I say lazily. We're both on our stomachs with our heads resting on our arms, facing each other. "I don't really see my mum and I have no siblings."

"I am lucky," she admits. "I complain, but secretly, I love it. I love all of them. And Malia does have a family. You're part of us now."

I smile sadly. "This is temporary. Riggs doesn't want me around to remind him of the war I've caused for his club. Cree looks like he wants to stab me every time he sees me."

"You're wrong," says Leia. "My brother would not go to war without good reason. He must think you're worth it. I haven't seen him so invested in a woman since . . . well . . . why don't you see your mum?" she asks.

"We don't get on. I grew up in care, and by the time I was sent back to live with her, we were resentful of each other. She didn't want me there, but my aunt forced the issue, I think. I was at that age where I thought everyone was against me and I sensed she didn't want me around."

"What happened to your aunt?"

I roll onto my back and close my eyes. "She passed away. Cancer. I think it was her dying wish to see us together because I came home at fifteen and she died six months later."

"That's sad," mutters Leia. "Here at the club, I have loads of aunts, Non-blood related though." She laughs. "You kind of forget who's a blood relation when you all live under one roof."

"I have trouble remembering everyone's name," I say. I open one eye. "Obviously, I know your mum, Frankie. The only other one that I remember is Bonnie and that's because I helped her get your brother to bed a few nights ago when he was drunk."

"Drunk?" asks Leia, raising her head slightly to look at me.

"Yeah. The first night I was here. She struggled to get him up the stairs."

"The last time I saw Riggs drunk was after Michelle left with Ziggy. He was broken."

"Why did she leave?" I ask.

A shadow falls over us. "You wanna know shit like that, you can come and ask me." Riggs' gruff voice washes over me and I realize I've spent the last few days missing it.

"I would, but you're never around," I say. "So, why did Michelle leave?" I only ask because he's clearly caught me, and I feel embarrassed. I try to pass off a carefree expression like I've done nothing wrong.

"None of your business," he mutters. "Leia, can you spend some time with Ziggy and Michelle? I've got church and she wants to spend time with him, but he still doesn't want to be alone with her."

Leia nods. "Of course." She stands and pulls a t-shirt on over her bikini. "See you later, Anna."

"I don't appreciate you digging for information," he grates out.

"I wasn't," I protest. "We were just talking."

"You were talking about me. Don't." He's so cold and expressionless that my heart sinks. This is how he was the first night I met him. "Your husband is causing me some real problems, Anna. He's sent his thugs in to smash up my bar."

I stand. "The Windsor? Shit."

"He's taken full advantage of us all being here." He makes his way back towards the club and I follow.

"So, what happens now?"

"I get a plan together. Don't worry about it."

"What about visiting on Sunday? He'll want to see Malia."

Riggs stops suddenly, causing me to crash into his back. My hands go to his waist and I feel the energy the mument our skin touches. I drop my hands and step back. "Are you fucking insane? You can't take Malia to see him."

"But there's a court order. I'll be breaking it."

"That's the least of your worries. You leave here and he won't let you come back. You'll be dead and he'll have Malia to himself."

"If I stop him from seeing his daughter, I'll be dead anyway."

"What's really going on here, Anna?" he growls. He steps closer and I back up until I hit the side of the building. The bricks scratch against my back. "Do you want to take Malia so she can see him or is it you who needs to see him?"

"I don't want to see him," I say. "But he'll make my life hell if I don't go."

He laughs sarcastically. "He's already making your life hell. You've come to a point now where your choice is hell or death. I've given you a third option. Don't fuck it up for the sake of a visit."

He's so close, I can smell the bourbon on his breath. His eyes fall to my breasts and I'm very aware of my nakedness and the fact that my chest is rising and falling at a rapid rate. "I'm offering you your life back. One for you and Malia. It doesn't include Reggie. If that's not what you want, then say it now before I go into church and plan his downfall."

I swallow and his eyes move to my throat. "Church?" I whisper. "You go to church?"

His mouth comes closer and I hold my breath in anticipation of a kiss. *Oh god, I want him to kiss me so badly.*

"It's not that kind of church, darlin'. Put some fucking clothes on before you go back in there or I'll end up killing my own brothers." His eyes sweep over me one last time and then he's gone. The door slams closed, and I release the breath I'm holding.

Chapter 12

RIGGS

I wait for my brothers to settle around the large oak table. Cree sits to my left and Chains to my right. My VP and Enforcer want Reggie's blood, but it's a decision we have to make as a club. When everyone is seated, I bang the gavel on the table and silence falls across the room. "You all know why we're here. The Windsor is a fucking mess. I went to see Pinky earlier today, and she escaped with cuts and bruises, but fuck is she mad."

"She's a tough bird," says Trucker, and we all nod in agreement.

"Damn right," I say. "She was cleaning up when I was there, determined to open up again as soon as."

"But that's not the point," snaps Cree. "Reggie can't get away with this. It's a direct hit to the club, and if we don't act, then we look weak."

"Pres, is this girl really worth it?" asks Rock and all eyes turn to him and then come back to me, waiting to see my reaction.

I tap my fingers on the table. "Reggie is using Anna to start the war. It's an excuse. From what I hear, he's got a new piece of ass living with him. Reggie would have begun the war with or without Anna being involved. He tried to get Marshall Ankers to take his business over the tracks. Marshall is one of our biggest dealers. If he took his supply from the docks, it would have an impact on our income."

"Are you claiming Anna?" asks Blade.

"Why all the fucking questions about Anna?" I snap. "This is about Reggie. I'm paying him a visit. Going to his side of the tracks to let him know we aren't scared. Everyone who's in, say I." I look around the table and one by one the brothers vote. Once I have everyone's vote, I bang the gavel to mark the end of church. Looks like I'm paying that motherfucker a visit.

We pour out of church and Bonnie's waiting for me. I try to hide my annoyance. "I don't have time now, Bonnie. We'll talk tonight."

"That's what you've been saying for the last few nights, and each time you fall to sleep. I want clarity. I need to know what you want," she snaps.

I nod and give her a chaste kiss on the cheek. "Later." Anna watches us from her seat on the couch, too far away to hear what was said. As I pass her, she makes eye contact.

"Did you come up with a plan?"

"Club business, sorry."

"It involves me," she says, looking puzzled.

"It involves your husband. I don't know if you plan on telling him what's going on," I say, and the mument the words leave my mouth, I regret them. I know she'd never tell Reggie anything, and the hurt shows on her face. She holds out her Mobile to me. "I don't want that," I mutter.

"Take it. No one calls me on it anyway apart from him. Take it and you'll see that I never respond to him. He texts me every day and I never respond."

I take her Mobile, not because I don't trust her but because I want to see what the messages say that he sends her. I tuck it into my back pocket. "I have to go. I didn't mean that. I trust you," I add, but she doesn't reply.

I kick the stand down on my bike and look back as my brothers park up behind me. I pull out Anna's Mobile and check through the messages while I wait for the brothers to gather. There are messages from Reggie, mainly asking her to answer his calls, but Anna was right, she didn't reply to him.

Reggie's hangout is a casino. We cross the street, and as we get closer to the doorway of The Casino, one of the security team steps forward. He takes one look at the patch on my kutte and shakes his head. I don't give him a chance to speak before my fist connects with his face, then I grip his head and pull his face down to connect with my knee. He falls to the ground and I head inside, leaving one of my guys to take care of him.

It's still early, so the place isn't busy. I know exactly where Reggie will be because we've met here before. He looks up from his Mobile as we approach. He smiles wide and relaxes back in his chair. "Who knew you had so many friends," he quips.

I sit down in the chair opposite him. Another of his security team steps forward, but Reggie shakes his head and he steps back into the shadows. "You should think about upping your security," I say.

Reggie glances over at the twenty or so bikers positioning themselves around us. "And you should really think about downsizing. How will you ever take anyone by surprise with a whole load of buffoons behind you?"

"I don't go in for surprise. I'm more of an upfront kinda guy. When I come for you, I want you to see me."

"Tragic news about your bar," he says and smiles. "Hope no one was injured."

"I don't think you've thought things through, Reg."

He laughs. "Says the person who walked into my casino."

"This is me showing you I'm not fucking scared and I'm not bringing her back to you. I'm keeping her and Malia." I smirk.

Reggie's fists tighten and his jaw ticks. "Then be prepared for me to rip your town apart, brick by brick, person by person, until Anna is back by my side."

"Why do you want her so bad, Reggie? I hear you have a pretty blond hanging off your arm these days. What's the big deal?"

He leans forwards and a smile plays on his lips. "Now, if you'd have fucked my wife, you'd know exactly why I want her back. All the blonds in the world cannot take her place."

"You'd still want her back knowing I've been there?" I ask with a laugh.

"It doesn't matter to me. I miss the way her pussy grips my cock and the noises she makes when she comes. I could beat her with one hand and fuck her with the other and she'd still come. I miss biting the tattoo of my name right next to her . . . " He grins. "Well, I'm sure you've seen it."

I keep my poker face in check. "It's been a nice chat, Reg. Now we're clear where we stand, the war can begin."

As I walk away, he shouts out, "The war has already begun, Riggs."

I drag my arm across the bar as I leave, knocking the freshly washed glasses to the ground. The crashing sound fills me with pleasure.

I stay sitting on my bike when we arrive back at the club. It's getting dark and I like the peace and quiet that the early evening brings. I light up a cigarette and stare up at the sky.

"I know I wasn't keen in the beginning," says Cree, standing by my bike. "But you're going to all this trouble, it makes me wonder what your intentions are with Anna."

I rub a hand over my beard. "Shit, man, I've fucked up."

"Why?"

"I tried it on with Bonnie the other night. Luckily, I was so drunk that I passed out, but that wasn't before I practically begged her to fuck me." Cree laughs hard and I groan. "It ain't funny, brother."

"So that's why she's desperate to talk?"

"Yeah. I reckon I said some crazy shit about trying to make things work and taking things to the next level. I'm usually so controlled and I blew it in one fucking night."

"Don't be so hard on yourself, man. You didn't fuck her and you're not with Anna, so technically you didn't do anything wrong."

I nod. "I know, but I told Anna to trust me. I told her there was nothing like that between me and Bonnie."

"I find it hilarious that you've spent years single and now three women are at the click of your fingers," he says.

"I hope you're not including me in those three women," comes Anna's voice. Cree smirks, and I punch his shoulder and mutter what a dick he is.

Bonnie appears behind Anna and I groan. *Like this couldn't get much worse.* "I'm waiting for you," snaps Bonnie. "Do you wanna talk out here or in bed?"

"Get it over and done with," whispers Cree.

I get off my bike and flick the cigarette butt to the ground, crushing it under my boot. As I pass Anna, we stare at each other but don't speak. I decide I'll put this right with Bonnie and then pursue Anna. I need her and I know deep down she feels the same.

Bonnie sits on the bed. "Look," I begin, "I was really drunk the other night."

"Oh shit. You're gonna go back on everything you said," she hisses. "You bastard."

"My life is fucking complicated, Bonnie. I don't have time for relationships. It wouldn't be fair to you."

"Jesus, if you're gonna back out, at least be fucking honest," she spits. "You've been eye-fucking Anna since the day she strolled into The Windsor. It's clear you're hot for her."

"She doesn't feel the same way, so that's not the issue."

"Well, don't think I'm spending another night in your bed. All those weeks of lying there with you when I could have been working my magic on one of the other guys." She stands and heads for the door. "You're an ass."

I look at the large empty bed. I won't get much sleep tonight. I'm too amped up after my visit to Reggie, and now that Bonnie's gone, I'll never be able to relax enough. I head down to the office, deciding to work through the night.

My vision is blurred, but it's almost sunrise. I pour another cup of coffee as the kitchen door opens and Anna creeps in. When she spots me, she shrieks in fright and then grips her chest. "Fuck," she pants.

"What are you doing up at . . . " I check my watch. "Four-thirty."

"I couldn't sleep," she whispers.

"You don't have to whisper. This place sleeps better than the dead. We sometimes throw parties until six in the morning and the kids manage to sleep through them." I pull out the milk pan and pour in some milk. "Sit," I say, nodding to a chair.

"Why are you up so early?"

"Up early or awake late." I shrug. "I can't sleep."

"Because of Bonnie?" she asks quietly. I turn to look at her for an explanation. "I overheard her telling one of the ol' ladies that you'd dumped her. She wasn't very happy."

"I was never with her, so it's hardly a break-up." I spoon some honey into the milk and stir it until it boils.

"Girls always read too much into things. She's been sharing your bed. In her head, that made her close to becoming your ol' lady," she says. I pour the hot milk into a mug and hand it to her. "How did it go with Reggie?"

I take the seat next to her and sip my coffee. "He knows you're not going home."

"I'm not?" she asks. I shake my head. "What did he say to that?"

"Don't worry about him. I'll deal with him."

"Club business," she says, throwing my words back from earlier.

"No," I mutter, shaking my head. "I just don't want *you* to worry. That's my job." We fall quiet for a few minutes, both sipping our drinks. "Did he hit you a lot?" I ask.

Anna chews on her lower lip and then nods. "Eva doesn't know the extent. I felt stupid because I stayed so long. Then every time I left, he'd force me back."

"Something he said tonight got in my head," I mutter. The thought of him beating her and then having sex makes me sick to my stomach.

As if reading my mind, she shakes her head. "I didn't enjoy anything he did to me. He'd say I did. It was my body's reaction to sex, I guess," she trails off. "Shit, this isn't the kind of talk for four-thirty in the morning."

"I don't get men who hit women like that. Why do they beat on a woman to make themselves feel powerful?"

"Reggie's cruel. His words, his actions, things he'd force me to do— he's just cruel. He likes to show me that I'm not in control, he is. He likes pain, inflicting it. It gets him off," she explains. I groan. I don't need that image in my head. "He would cut me and enjoy that I was in pain." She sighs and takes a drink of her milk. "You asked Bonnie for skin," she says, staring down into her mug. "You told me that you never had sex with her, but then I heard you tell her that you needed to feel her skin against yours."

I cringe. I hate that she heard that. "I didn't lie to you, Anna. I wouldn't. I was drunk that night. I said some stupid shit to her, but I swear I never meant a word of it. I didn't lay a finger on her, and I've spoken to her. That's why she was pissed earlier. I told her straight that we weren't ever gonna happen like that."

"So, there's nothing going on with you and her?" she asks, and I shake my head in response. "Why did Michelle leave?" she adds.

"I cheated on her," I say, looking her directly in the eyes. "I cheated over and over. Broke her heart and she turned to drugs. Turns out, they made her happier than I did. Growing up in this life is hard. I watched the guys with the club whores. It's just part of it. I was a horny young teenager and girls were throwing themselves at me. I was gonna be the club's next president and every girl wanted to be my ol' lady. Michelle didn't." I smile at the memory of Michelle in college. "I liked that about her. There were no expectations for me to make her part of the club, but she fell into it and she fitted in here. I loved her, so fucking much." The usual pain that I get when I think about my relationship with Michelle squeezes my heart. "But I thought it was okay to cheat. She was pregnant and wasn't interested in sex. I stupidly thought that mattered. Fuck, I was such an ass."

"How did she find out?" she asks.

"Club whores talk. I guess it just got back to her. She stayed, and when she confronted me, I admitted it. I blamed it all on her because that's the kind of dick I'd become, but she stuck around for Ziggy's sake. The club was her support. We tried to make it work, but I loved the other life too much. I pushed her over the edge."

"That's why you help her out? Your mum told me you buy her groceries and check in on her." I nod. "I think that's sweet. You recognize what you did was fucked up and you're trying to make up for it."

"It's not enough though. She's not ready to get better. I've got Blade bringing that shit into her so she doesn't leave to look for it. How messed up is that?"

Anna places her hand over mine and smiles. "If it keeps her safe, then it's what you have to do."

I turn my hand and take her fingers in mine, gently caressing the back of her hand. "So, what about after Michelle?" she asks.

"After?" I repeat. "There's been no one after."

She laughs and rolls her eyes in disbelief. "Yeah, right."

"I'm being honest. After Michelle, I re-evaluated my life. Of course, I've had sex, but nothing meaningful, and for the last year or so, I've not bothered chasing club whores. It becomes too much hassle. They all want to become your ol' lady."

"Hold on," she laughs. "So, you're telling me you haven't had sex for the last year?" Hearing it out loud makes me cringe. If the guys overheard, they'd think I was a pussy. "Why not?"

I shrug my shoulders. "I was sick of the same old shit. Drinking. Sex. It became boring. I've been concentrating on the club."

"Shit," she gasps. "So, when you . . . " She blushes. "Yah know . . . " She points between her legs and I grin. "Didn't you want to . . . " She pauses and blushes again.

"Fuck you?" I ask, and she nods. "Of course, I did, but I've become an expert at controlling myself." She stares at me wide-eyed.

Chapter 13

ANNA

I'm staring at him like a deer caught in headlights. I'm shocked and amazed. I didn't expect him to confess that. Without thinking, I throw myself towards him and press my lips against his. I'm so turned on by his confession that I completely take the lead and push myself to stand between his legs. I run my fingers over his stubbly cheeks and kiss him as if my life depends on it. This time, when I feel his erection pressing into my stomach, I rub my hand over the material of his jeans. I keep my mouth against his and reach for his belt. When he doesn't stop me, I rip it open. He stands and I pop the buttons on his pants and push them down his thighs. "Shit, Anna, I feel like a fucking teenager," he mutters.

I stare down at his impressive erection and lick my lips. I lower to my knees and Riggs grips the stool behind him. I notice his knuckles turn white and smile to myself. The tip of his penis glistens and I rub my thumb over the droplet. I pop the digit into my mouth and Riggs groans. I take his cock in my hand with a firm grip and run my tongue over the head. His eyes are half-closed as he watches me run my tongue up and down his length. When I finally take him in my mouth, he hisses and stiffens. I push him to the back of my throat until I can't take him any further. I make sure my eyes connect with his as I slowly release him before repeating it again.

I move my hand in sync with my mouth and Riggs throws his head back. I cup his balls and his body shudders.

Suddenly, he grips my hand and pulls me to stand. We stare at each other, the sound of our panting breaths filling the room.

"Why don't you let go for once," I whisper. "Lose control." Riggs shakes his head and I smirk. He hasn't moved away, so I see it as a challenge and reach out for his erection. I grip him again and begin to pump my hand back and forth. He closes his eyes like he's enjoying it, but after a few seconds, he stops me again. I shimmy out of my pyjama shorts and then lift my vest over my head. He looks torn up when he sees I'm completely naked underneath. He's scared to let go after so long of controlling himself, but then he allows his eyes to roam over my body.

This man is putting everything on the line for me. *Why have I held back this long?*

He scrubs a hand over his face and tugs on his beard. "Say it," he mutters. "I see it in your eyes, but I want to hear you say the words."

I don't hesitate in my reply. "Fuck me," I whisper.

The moan that slips from his lips sounds pained. He pulls me by the waist and lifts me effortlessly onto the kitchen worktop. He steps between my legs and holds my face at an angle, kissing me hard and fast. In a low, gravelly voice, he says, "If we do this, I can't let you go, Anna."

I nod and he presses his forehead against mine. "I mean it. You understand what I'm saying, right? We're together from the second we step over that line." I nod again. "Words," he grits out.

"I get it. I'm yours," I say. He growls and kisses me again. "I'm on the pill," I add, wriggling against him impatiently and he smiles against my lips.

His forehead rests against mine again and he looks down between us. I feel him nudging at my entrance and he gently pushes forward, entering me slowly. I cry out as he stretches me. It feels so amazing and the delicious warm feeling I've craved since I set eyes on him begins to build. I wrap my arms around his neck and run my tongue over his lower lip until he grants me entrance and our mouths crash together.

He pushes in as far as my body will allow and then inches out. He stills, looking back down between us, and then he slams hard into me. I cry out again, shivering against him. I feel his fingers dig into my ass as he pulls me from the counter. I have no control, and he moves me against him in a way that builds up my orgasm with such speed that it crashes through me, catching me off guard. My whole body shakes and quivers, and he doesn't let up his punishing pace until he's grunting in my ear. It's the sexiest sound I've ever heard, and as I feel him stiffen, he roars. His legs shake and he squeezes my ass, trying to get as deep into me as he can.

"Fuckkkkkk," he mutters. He stills and rests his head against my chest.

"Was it what you expected after a year of abstaining?" I ask with a smile. He lowers me to my feet, and I notice his cock is still semi-hard. He turns me away from him and bends me over the worktop. He lines himself up at my entrance again and pushes inside me.

"It was better," he pants. "But I'm not done yet." He begins to fuck me— like, really fuck me. I try to grab onto the edge of the worktop to stop from slipping over the other side. Riggs presses his body over my back and that seems to hold me in place as he slams into me. "It's gonna be a long day," he mutters, placing his hands over me and holding onto the edge of the worktop to give himself more leverage.

I don't know how long we fuck like that, but I orgasm twice before he stills and shudders against me. I'm hot and my body glistens with sweat. Riggs pulls out of me. "Stay there," he whispers. I watch him go through the cupboards until he finds a new dishcloth. He wets in the basin and then stands behind me and gently cleans between my legs. I blush, not used to being taken care of.

He helps me to stand and then crouches down in front of me and holds my shorts open so I can step into them. He helps me into my vest and then throws the dishcloth into the waste bin. "You need sleep," he whispers. He takes my hand and leads me from the kitchen and up to my bedroom. My head is spinning, and my entire body feels like it's floating.

He stops at the doorway and I see that Malia is still sound asleep. "Aren't you sleeping?" I ask. He shakes his head and places a kiss on my head. "G'night," I whisper.

"Goodnight," he says and smiles. He waits for me to go inside and close the door. I can't stop the satisfied grin from forming on my face. I feel so relaxed and happy. I don't want to jinx it, but I feel like I can finally begin to see a future for me and Malia.

I sleep for another two hours before Malia wakes me. Nothing can dampen my mood today and I practically skip down to the kitchen hand-in-hand with Malia to make her breakfast. Frankie is already cooking bacon. Riggs is at the head of the table reading the newspaper, Ziggy is stuffing choco pops into his mouth, and Michelle is watching the pair fondly. Malia sits next to Ziggy and I fill her bowl with the same cereal because they have to have everything the same. I smile when I feel Riggs' fingers gently brush the skin at the back of my legs.

"Can't we at least go for a walk?" asks Michelle.

"Nope. I'm not discussing this, Michelle. Not in front of Ziggy," says Riggs firmly. His hand moves up my leg and rests on my ass. Michelle notices and her face hardens slightly.

"A walk in the park is hardly a death sentence. Nothing's happened, and whoever you've upset probably doesn't even know who I am. Ziggy's my son too and I want to spend time with him."

"Really," scoffs Frankie, placing a plate of bacon and pancakes on the table. "You're gonna go there?"

"I will not discuss this in front of the kids," says Riggs and I hide my smile. I like the way he's including Malia by saying 'kids'. "Now, shut the hell up and let me eat my breakfast. I had a busy night."

Michelle stomps out of the kitchen and Riggs tugs my hand until I lower into the seat next to him. "You didn't get any sleep?" I ask quietly. He shakes his head. "Will you sleep later?" He shakes his head again. "Because you don't have someone lying with you?" I ask. He stares at me but doesn't confirm or deny the reason. "Maybe we can catch a nap later if Eva could watch the kids?" He grins and nods his head.

Riggs has work to do, so I go in search of Eva. I find her in her bedroom. It's similar to the one I'm staying in— bright and airy. She smiles from her spot on the bed as she turns the page of a book.

"You're looking mighty happy with yourself. You have a glow about you," she says with a smile. "Does that have anything to do with a certain tattooed, hot biker who goes by the name of Pres?"

I bite on my lower lip and smile coyly. "Maybe."

Eva sits up and pats the bed, and I sit down. "I need details," she demands.

I close my eyes and groan. "Eva, he's so hot!"

"That, I know. I want info about the bits I can't see." She grins.

"Let's just say I think I had more orgasms last night than I ever had with Reggie for the entire time we were together." We fall into a fit of giggles. "What about you and Cree?"

"I don't know why everyone keeps asking me that. mum asked the same thing over breakfast. Cree isn't into me like that," she says.

I roll my eyes. "How the hell do you not see it? Come with me, I'll show you." I take her hand and we go downstairs to the main room. It's a little quieter today. People must be hiding out in their rooms or outside. Cree is at the same table as yesterday, with his laptop open, and he's frowning down at a pile of papers. Gears and another biker are by the pool table and I pull Eva in their direction. "I wish I could play pool," I sigh. "Are you guys too busy to show us?" I add, sounding hopeful.

Gears shrugs at the other guy and then smiles. "I guess we have time for you gorgeous ladies. I'll take you, new girl," he says to me. He's called me that since my first day at the garage.

"Lake, that's Eva." Lake steps back and looks Eva up and down with a grin on his face.

"Pleasure's all mine," he grits out and kisses Eva on the cheek. I spot Cree looking up at the mention of Eva's name. "I haven't seen you around here before."

"She's with me," I say.

"Well, for now, she's with me." Lake stands behind her and shows her how to hold the pool cue. She bends over the table and I know those shorts she's wearing must be riding up enough to show some of her ass. Lake presses himself over her, helping her to line up the cue.

Cree growls and grips the edge of his table. His eyes are burning into the back of Lake's head. I smile to myself. They pot the ball and Eva jumps around in delight. Lake's eyes fix to her chest and I see Cree grit his jaw.

"Come on, new girl. It's your turn," says Gears, positioning himself behind me. I'd underestimated how up close and personal the guys needed to be as he bends me over the table. I'm so flustered that I miss the shot.

Lake waits for Eva to bend over before sidling up behind her and gripping her hips. Eva sucks in a surprised breath and Cree stands so suddenly that his chair tips back and crashes to the ground. We all look over as Cree stares back, his nostrils flared and his chest heaving. He resembles a bull about to charge. Lake drops his hands from Eva and swallows hard. "You okay, VP?" he asks.

"Eva," he growls as she hands the cue to Lake. "What did I say to you?"

"Erm," she mumbles, and her cheeks flush.

"Stay away from my brothers," he reminds her. "Get out of my sight." Eva glances at me.

I'm aware of Gears still holding onto me by the waist and I'm about to drag Eva back to her room so we can discuss this situation when an almighty roar comes from the office doorway.

"What the fuck is going on?" yells Riggs as he marches towards us.

Gears holds up his hands in the air where they can be seen. "Pres, I was showing her how to play," he rushes out with panic lacing his words. "Nothing in it, I swear." Riggs is already in his face. "Pres, I swear," he repeats.

"Christ, Riggs, calm down," I hiss, embarrassed that this whole thing got out of hand. He slowly turns his head in my direction and I almost wilt under his intense glare.

"'Scuse me?" he utters.

"We were playing pool. No big deal," I say.

"And that was a reason to be touching each other?" Before I can come up with a smart answer, he grabs me by the wrist and marches me upstairs. "Eva, watch the kids," he throws over his shoulder.

Riggs pulls me into his room, then slams and locks the door. I stand awkwardly in the middle of the room. "I think that was a little OTT," I mutter.

He stands behind me and grabs a handful of my hair. He gently tugs my head back, exposing my neck to his mouth. "I don't want to see any other man's hands on your body," he hisses in my ear. He nips his way down my neck and along my shoulder. "I told you, once we fuck, that's it, we're together. No one can touch what's mine." I shudder at his words. They should scare me after what Reggie put me through, but they don't. They make me feel all kinds of safe. He runs his other hand under my top and wraps it around my waist, pulling me against his strong, hard body. "I told you lack of sleep makes me crazy."

"I was helping Eva see that Cree likes her," I admit weakly. "It went wrong."

"No shit, Sherlock," he mutters. "You should never piss off two of the most hot-headed males in this place. It'll get someone killed." He flicks the button on my denim shorts and then eases them down my legs using one hand. The other remains in my hair. "You wanna learn to play, you ask me."

"I know how to play pool," I sigh. "I wanted to get a reaction from Cree." He pushes me to bend at the waist so that my hands rest on the bed. I jump when he brings his hand down hard on my naked ass.

"So, you let Gears touch you even though you knew how to play?" he growls. I hesitate before I answer, and he slaps my ass again.

"I admit it wasn't a well thought out plan. I think it's lack of sleep," I mutter weakly.

Riggs runs a hand between my legs, and I cry out. "You're wet," he whispers, and I hear the smile in his voice. "You like to be punished?"

"By you," I whisper, and he groans.

"So, you're not wet like this for Gears?" He spanks me again.

"No," I hiss. His hand goes back to teasing me and I shudder.

"I should make him watch while I fuck you," he growls, rubbing more vigorously. I feel an orgasm building and I begin to squirm. I'm not sure if I'm trying to get more friction or less, but I can't hold still, and as the first waves hit me, Riggs places his free arm across my back to hold me down. He doesn't slow the pace of his rubbing and I scream as the warm rush hits me hard.

Riggs doesn't wait for me to recover. He pushes his jeans just below his ass and then slams into me hard. I grip the sheets. "Fuck," he growls. "I think your pussy was made for me."

My legs are weak and I'm pretty certain I may pass out if he makes me come again. He grabs hold of my shoulders and pulls me to stand. He pins my arms behind my back and turns me slightly so that we're looking into his floor-length mirror. My breasts are jutting out and my cheeks are flushed pink. Riggs' body fills the mirror and I look petite compared to his huge build. The tattoos that cover his chest and arms make my tanned skin look pale. Seeing him looking so strong and alpha like this drives me crazy. His eyes lock onto mine in the mirror. "Fuckin' beautiful," he growls against my ear.

I begin to shudder. "Riggs," I pant. "I can't . . . "

"Finn," he hisses. "Call me Finn."

"Finn," I repeat, and he closes his eyes briefly. "Finn." This time it comes out shaky. "I can't come again," I moan.

"The fuck you can't," he hisses. "I want to feel you squeezing my cock." He moves one hand to my front and pinches my nipple. I cry out again. "Come on my cock, Anna," he growls.

My legs almost fall from under me as my body shakes uncontrollably. I have no choice as the climax rips me apart. Riggs spits out a string of curses as he follows me over the edge. He looks down to where we're joined, and his face stiffens when he finally comes inside of me. He thrusts hard with a grunt and then stills.

After a few seconds, he releases me and points to the bed. "Sleep," he mutters.

"I need to clean up," I say, but he shakes his head and jostles me over to the bed where he throws the sheets to one side. I climb in and he follows me.

He pulls me against him, and I feel his semi-erect cock against my ass. "I feel gross," I point out.

"How can it be gross?" he mumbles sleepily. "It's us mixed together."

Chapter 14

RIGGS

I wake up disorientated. My cock is painfully hard, and I feel too hot. I glance at my watch. It's almost six in the evening. We must have slept most of the damn day. Anna stirs beside me, but before she can fully wake up, I push into her. She moans and I smile. I love hearing her moan when she's full of me.

I planned on slow, sleepy sex, but something primal takes over and I find myself climbing over her and settling back between her legs before slamming into her. She wakes fully and her hands reach above her head to grip the headboard. "Hold on, baby," I warn and then I let the animal in me take her hard and fast. We fuck, and it's not long before I come again on a roar. I slow down and reach between us to rub her swollen clit until she comes too.

I fall down beside her. "Shit, what is it about you?" I mutter more to myself than her. "You've bewitched me."

"I think it's you who's bewitched me. I bet Eva is cursing me. I hope the kids have been good," she says.

"We'll take them away for a few days when I can lift the lockdown," I say. "Ziggy loves the sea."

"What are you gonna do about Reggie?" she asks quietly.

"I told you already, it's not your concern." I sit up and pull myself to the edge of the bed. "If you're gonna be my ol' lady, then you have to understand that I can't talk about that shit with you."

"Maybe if you offloaded, you'd sleep better," she suggests.

"I offload to Cree. I offload to my brothers. But I look after you," I say firmly. "It's just the way it is."

"Then change it. You're the president. Don't you make the rules?" she asks.

"Yes, but this rule stays because I want it to. I wanna take care of you, Anna. Some of the shit I do . . . " I pause and sigh. "You don't need those images in your head. The women here, they don't ask questions. If I come home covered head to toe in blood, you shower with me and fuck me. That's how you help me."

She sits up and wraps the sheet around her. "Sounds old fashioned. This isn't the eighteen-hundreds. Women have equal rights these days. I've looked after myself since I was a kid," she points out.

I laugh, shaking my head. "And a fine job you did of that," I say sarcastically. Anna glares at me and her eyes almost bug out of her head. "Sorry," I sigh. "I shouldn't have said that."

"No. Please, speak your mind. Don't hold back," she snaps.

"Anna, I didn't mean it. I'm not used to being questioned."

"So you want a doormat? One that doesn't question you? You want me to sit, looking pretty, and smile at all your jokes? Fuck you when you seem upset or stressed? Wash the blood from your clothes, but if I step out of my box, you'll throw my past at me?"

"Anna," I sigh.

"No, Riggs," she snaps, getting up from the bed. "I just want to clarify what you need from me." I remain silent. Whatever I say to her right now, she'll lose her mind. She's raging. "What if you seem mad but I don't know why, can I ask what's wrong or is that above my station? Am I allowed to enquire about how you're feeling?" she rants.

"You're blowing this out of proportion," I say calmly.

"I don't think I am," she mutters. She begins picking her clothes up from the floor.

"Where are you going?"

"I spent years with a man who wanted a Barbie doll on his arm. I was good enough to open my legs but not to speak for myself. I was good enough to attend his business dinners and look good beside him, but if I asked the wrong thing, I'd become his punchbag."

"I'm not the fucking same as that piece of shit," I growl.

"No?" she asks. "Maybe you're more alike than you think. You call it looking after me, I call it controlling me. He called it love, I called it abuse. At the end of the day, you both want a woman who bows down to you and doesn't ask any questions. I won't be that person again."

I let her leave the bedroom even though everything inside of me says to stop her, to pin her down and make her listen to me. At least she can't go anywhere outside the club, and if I've learned anything about women, it's to leave them to cool off.

"What did you do?" Cree smirks as he joins me at the bar a couple of hours later.

"What are you talking about?" I ask.

"If things could get any frostier between you and Anna, we'd be on the film set to *Frozen* . And before you say a word, I only know about *Frozen* because Ziggy makes me watch it."

"Yeah, of course he does. Funny ass," I mutter. He's right. Anna hasn't spoken two words to me all evening. The kids wanted to have a sleepover in Ziggy's room, and we were both in there to tuck them in, but she wouldn't even look at me. "I made some comment and she blew it up. How do women have the ability to do that?"

"Beats me. I don't have that issue. Maybe try and talk less, like me. Just growl and boss her around instead."

I roll my eyes. "I don't think Anna's a boss around type of woman. She growls more than me. What happened with you and Eva earlier?"

"You're doing it again," groans Cree. "Stop trying to talk about emotions and shit."

"You know it's normal for people to talk like this, right? It's only you who hates it and tries to make a big deal out of it. Anna set you up earlier. That little display with Gears and Lake was to get a reaction from you. She's tryin' to prove you got feelings for Eva."

Cree stares down at his beer. "Something about Eva drives me wild," he admits. "I haven't had that before."

"Like you'd do anything to protect her?" I ask, understanding exactly the feelings he's talking about. "You wanna make all their decisions so that you know they're safe."

Cree nods his head. "Yeah, something like that. Seeing Lake's hands on her . . . " he trails off and I pat him sympathetically on the back. "But I don't want anything to happen like that. I can't do the ol' lady bullshit."

"Then there's every chance she may end up with some other guy," I point out and he clenches his jaw.

"I told her to stay away from the brothers. Once all this shit with Reggie is done, she can go back to her life and I don't have to see her again. If it ain't under my nose, then I won't know either way."

I nod over to where Lake is chatting with Eva and Anna. "Maybe you should warn the brothers that she's off-limits."

I drink way more than I should . . . again. I sit by the bar watching the brothers party, my eyes seeing double vision and my head spinning. I make out Bonnie approaching me. She's ignoring me too. Seems to be a trend around here lately. She stands by me trying to get the prospect's attention. "You still ignoring me?" I slur.

"Just getting myself a drink, Pres," she mutters.

"It's not you," I continue. "I mean . . . " I look down at her ass. "I'd love nothing more than to sink into that fine ass, but I—"

"Oh my god," screeches Anna, and I groan. My blurry eyes make out her angry face. Her hands are on her hips and she looks pissed. "We have one disagreement and you're trying to jump into bed with Bonnie?"

"No, I wasn't. I just—"

"I heard what you were saying. You asshole!" She stomps away in the direction of the stairs. I go after her, stumbling into the walls, and I catch her at the bottom of the stairs. "Every time you drink, you end up back with Bonnie. How can I ever trust you?" she asks.

"I don't fucking want Bonnie. Anna, I love you," I blurt out. "Just you." I sigh. Anna stares at me. A range of emotions passes over her face. "Don't make me sleep alone," I add.

She takes a deep breath, but I think I see her face soften slightly. "We need some rules," she says firmly. I nod my head eagerly. I'll say anything right now just to have her smile at me. She takes me by the hand and leads me upstairs. "We're talking tomorrow, Riggs. I know you have rules around here, but I have boundaries and we need to compromise on a few things."

"Okay, we'll talk."

"And compromise," she pushes.

I follow her into my room. "Yes," I sigh. "And compromise."

The following day, I use avoidance tactics by bringing Anna breakfast in bed to begin with. She smiles as I place the tray on the bed. "How's your head?" she asks.

"Good. Eat up. I promised the kids we'd set up the paddling pool for them today and Frankie and Esther are making up enough picnic food to feed an army. Most of the club will be out in the yard today enjoying the sunshine."

She pulls herself to sit up. "But we're gonna talk, right, Riggs? We do need to talk."

I give her a chaste kiss on the lips. "Yeah, Angel. Later." I rush out before she can pin me here.

The next few days follow pretty much the same. We relax all day and fuck through the night. Whenever she tries to talk to me, I manage to change the subject with the promise that we'll talk soon. Truth is, I can't change the rules. I can't talk club business with her because I don't want it to touch her, to taint what we have. Our time together makes me feel so ridiculously happy that I want it to stay like this all the time. Hearing her laugh, seeing her smile, it makes all of this worthwhile. Even Malia is full of giggles. My brothers adore her, and she's settled right in as their little princess. It feels like we were always meant to be like this. Once Reggie is out of the way, I can make it official.

I stretch out in bed next to Anna. The sun shines through a gap in the drapes and I wince. My head is pounding. We drank way too much last night and my mouth feels like I've been licking sandpaper. I have a funny feeling in the pit of my stomach, and I sit up slowly. Anna rolls away from me, her naked body exposed as the sheet falls away. I lost count of the number of times I buried myself deep inside of her throughout the night. *There has to be a point where I stop wanting her so much, right?*

I take a shower and leave her to sleep. When I return, Malia is sitting on the bed playing with a doll. Anna smiles awkwardly. We hadn't spoken to the kids about us, but Malia obviously found her way here so maybe they just sensed it. "Ziggy not awake yet?" I ask. Usually, he's the first up around here.

"Yeah. He went with his mummy," says Malia as she runs a brush through her doll's hair. The funny feeling in my stomach ramps up a little.

"What do you mean?" I ask. "Went where?"

She shrugs and continues to play with the doll. Anna senses my unease and she places her hand over Malia's, stilling her. "Sweety, where did Ziggy go?" she asks.

"I think he went for breakfast," she says. We both visibly relax, and I smile. "Ziggy didn't want to go. She carried him and she said he would like the park because in the café they do ice cream."

I groan and my heart threatens to beat out of my chest at the possibility that Michelle took Ziggy for a walk outside of the clubhouse. "Don't panic. Maybe someone went with them," says Anna calmly.

"No," says Malia. "Ziggy's mummy told me not to tell you, but I don't like to tell lies."

I rush out of the room and take the stairs two at a time. Leia and my mum spin around alarmed when I burst into the kitchen. "Michelle . . . where's Michelle?" I'm desperate for them to tell me she's here somewhere, but they both stare at me blank. "She's got Ziggy," I add, and mum drops the bowl she was washing up into the basin. She dries her hands and follows me through the club, both of us shouting Ziggy's name.

I pull out my Mobile and call Michelle, but of course, it goes straight to the answer message. I curse and retry. Cree and Tiny are out in the yard. "You saw Michelle and Ziggy?" I ask. Cree shakes his head.

Tiny nods. "Yeah, she was around the back with him playing ball earlier when I was out guarding the gates. He was a little upset, if I'm honest, but she was really trying to make him happy." I don't listen to any more. Instead, I run around to the back of the club. Ziggy's ball lays on the grass, but they're nowhere to be seen. I call her Mobile over and over. When it finally rings on her end, I want to cry with relief. "Hello?" she answers.

"Get him back here now," I yell. "How dare you take him."

"Christ, Riggs, calm the fuck down," she hisses. "He's fine. We're just having an ice cream. You need to relax."

"The club is on lockdown for a fucking reason," I grit out. mum touches my arm, a silent warning for me to calm down.

I take a deep breath. "Where are you? I'll come and get you both."

"We're at the park. Literally around the corner. We'll head back. Yah know, I discussed this with your little girlfriend yesterday and she seemed fine with me taking Ziggy out." She disconnects the call.

Anna runs out into the yard just as I pull the Mobile away from my ear. "Are they okay?" she asks.

"Did you tell her she could take Ziggy?" I ask, moving towards her.

Anna shakes her head. "She mentioned it and I agreed with her that she should spend time with him. I never said that she could."

"Who do you think you are? You come along and think you can just take over and change the rules. You've been here two fuckin' minutes and you're making decisions about my kid?"

"No, I just—"

I'm filled with rage. Ziggy is my son and if she knew the shit that Michelle had put us through . . . "You had no right to get involved. We fucked. That doesn't mean you can involve yourself in shit between me and my ex. Ziggy is my responsibility. Concentrate on screwing your own kid up and leave mine alone."

Hurt fills Anna's face. "I didn't tell her she could take Ziggy out. I agreed she should spend time and get to know him. I told her to talk to you." Tears fall down her cheeks and she swipes at them angrily. "I would never get involved in your parenting decisions. Interesting that you say now we're just fucking. Is that all it's been?"

"Now's not the time to talk about us!" I growl.

"Oh, don't worry, I know you hate to talk. I think you've made yourself perfectly clear. All the picnics, the lazing around in the sun, the movie nights, all of those things this last week have meant nothing because we're just fucking, right?!" She turns and runs back inside.

I run my hands over my head. "Fuck," I groan. My heart aches and I can't shake the feeling of panic I feel over Ziggy being outside of the club.

"Jesus, Finn," mum mutters. "Do you think about the words before they come out of your mouth, or do you just blurt out that bullshit on the spot? You're just like your dad," she adds, then follows Anna inside.

I crouch down by the grass and hold my head in my hands. I was so terrified that something had happened to Ziggy that all that crap came rolling outta my mouth. Cree pats me on the shoulder. "Talk to her. Explain." He sighs.

I shake my head. "Yah know what, Cree, I don't think it'll work between us. I love her. How mad is that? I haven't known her long enough for that. We need to get this done with Reggie. Since those girls came into our lives, we've been fucking up all over the place. We've waited too long as it is because I've had my head full of her. Let's call church in an hour and put a plan together."

"Okay, but sort shit with Anna, Pres. I was wrong about her. Seeing you guys together these last few days, I've never seen you so happy."

"I thought you didn't talk about this sorta crap?" I mutter.

"Sometimes things need to be said. She's a good woman and you need her. Make it right." He goes inside. I'll make it right with Anna later. I have to get Ziggy back here first.

I pace by the gates. It's been six minutes since my call with Michelle and Ziggy still isn't back. I decide to walk to the park. Maybe Ziggy wanted to finish his ice cream there and it really is just around the corner.

When I arrive, I stand by the railings that surround the park. It's busy with families enjoying the warm weather. I pull out my Mobile and call her again. It rings out. I call mum to see if we've somehow missed each other and she's back there, but she isn't. I'll make sure she's never alone with Ziggy again after this stunt.

I jump the railings and make my way to the ice cream shack. There's no sign of them and the teenager behind the counter is no use, telling me he's seen a hundred mums with kids already today. I decide that maybe she took the long walk home, so I make my way back to the club. When I find that she still hasn't arrived there, I call her again. This time, a man answers, and I grip the Mobile tightly. If she's gone to buy drugs, I'll kill her myself.

"Where's Michelle?" I growl.

"I wanted your sister first," says the voice on the other end of the Mobile. "A virgin was worth the nights I had men sat outside your club waiting. But a crack whore and her brat will have to do."

My blood runs cold. Bile lingers in my throat. I'm holding the Mobile so tight, it threatens to crumble in my hand. "Reggie," I spit out.

"Hello again, Riggs. How's my wife?"

"You've no idea what you've done," I hiss.

"Oh, I have a very clear idea of what I'm doing. You thought you could take my wife and daughter, so now I have your girl and your son. Hurts, doesn't it?"

"What the fuck do you want?" I growl.

"You know what I want. I told you what would happen if she didn't return to me. One by one, I'll take everyone and everything she loves."

"This can't just be about them. What's so special that you'd hurt a child to get them back?" I growl.

"You're right. I want so much more. But we'll get to that after I have Anna and Malia back."

"I'm not returning fuck all until I have Ziggy home. You think I'm gonna return them and then listen to your demands?"

Reggie laughs. It's cold and cruel. "You don't have a choice, biker boy. At exactly noon, I'm gonna fuck your wife, and then every hour after that, I'll have my men fuck her. Nothing will be off-limits, and my men have very . . . interesting tastes. I should also point out that your son doesn't like the dark. He's making such a fuss down there. The quicker you get my wife home and agree to what I want, the quicker he'll see daylight again." The call disconnects and a noise escapes me. It's something between a scream and a wail. Ziggy hates being in the dark since living with Michelle and the thought of him crying for me tears me apart.

I lean over by the club gate and empty the contents of my stomach. It splatters over my boots. For the first time since my dad died, a tear rolls down my face. Chains spots me and rushes over. "Pres?" he asks.

"Get the brothers together," I mutter. I spit on the ground and then scrub my hands over my face. "And every goddamn weapon we own. I've got a war to win."

Chapter 15

ANNA

I stuff my belongings into my bags. "Just think about it. He was mad and he shouldn't have said what he did, but he didn't mean it. When it comes to Ziggy, he goes crazy protective," explains Frankie.

"I know. I get why he was mad. I would be too if he did that with Malia. We've had a great few days, Frankie." I pause, trying to stop the tears from falling again. "I really like him, and he just threw everything in my face. I was the one who kept my distance and he convinced me we were worth the risk. I've watched him with Malia this week and it's given me hope. Hope that we could be happy, all of us as a family."

"Baby girl, you can be." Frankie sighs, taking my hand. "You two were made for each other. I've never seen him smile so much. And it's not just me— everyone's saying the same thing. He loves you and I know you love him even if you don't see it yet. Please, stay. Talk to him."

"I promise I told Michelle to ask Riggs. I said it wasn't up to me. I could kick myself now. I was so fucking nice to her."

Frankie gives a look of disdain. "She's a nasty piece of work. I never liked her. She was sniffing around Finn like a hungry shark. Mothers know when their boys find trouble, and trust me, she had trouble written all over her. Finn will tell you a love story of how they fell in love after she got pregnant and how they tried to make it work, but I remember the arguments. She would wind him up by flirting with anything with a dick. If she could get attention, then she would play up for it. She'd twist situations and manipulate everyone. I caught her grinding up on Finn's dad once." Frankie shakes her head. "I should have kicked her ass then."

"I get the impression she really hurt him."

"The morning she left with Ziggy will be burnt into my brain forever. My boy was devastated. The distress stayed on his face for a solid year until he found them, and he never stopped looking. He brought Ziggy home and the poor kid was all bones. His skin was almost translucent because she was so high that she didn't bother to take him outside. Yah know, Ziggy still wets the bed because he's suffering from the trauma. I'll never forgive her for what she put my boys through."

I gently place my hand over hers and smile warmly. "They're lucky to have you, Frankie."

"That's why I know he'll be heartbroken when he realizes you've left. At least wait until he's calmed down so you can talk."

Leia bursts in. "mum, something happened to Ziggy," she pants. "The guys are in church, but Riggs wouldn't say what happened. He had that look on his face." Tears fill her eyes. "Like last time when Ziggy went missing."

"Michelle isn't back?" asks Frankie, and Leia shakes her head.

I follow them downstairs with my heart pounding hard in my chest. Frankie knocks on the door to church, but nobody bothers to answer. "I'm gonna go in," says Frankie.

Leia's eyes widen. "He'll go mental," she warns. "You know what he's like about rules."

Frankie shrugs and pushes the door open. "Fuck the rules." Twenty or so bikers fall silent and all eyes turn to us. In the centre of the large table are piles of guns, all different sizes. "Where's Ziggy?" asks Frankie.

The look on Riggs' face tells me something is very wrong. "Get out," he almost whispers.

"Finn—" begins Frankie.

"I said get the fuck out!" he yells, and we all jump with fright. Cree steps in front of us and carefully ushers us out of the room.

"I need to know, Cree," begs Frankie. "Is Ziggy okay?"

"We don't know. Reggie has them," he says. His eyes fall to me. "Now, go. We have plans to make."

I'm shaking as I step outside of the club. I pull out my Mobile and dial Reggie's number.

"Princess," he croons.

"What have you done?" I whisper. "This has nothing to do with them."

"It has everything to do with them. You made it their problem when you crossed onto their side of the tracks. You realize that you've unsettled years of peace between the Kings and my organization?"

"Please let them go, Reg," I beg. "I'm sorry, okay. I'll do whatever you want. Just let them go."

"You should have done what I wanted in the first place and then this war wouldn't have started." He sighs. "I'll send a driver to get you and Malia. Be ready in ten minutes."

He disconnects the call and I take a few deep breaths. I have to do this for Ziggy.

I go back inside the club, avoiding Frankie and Leia. Eva finds me in my bedroom, packing the rest of my stuff. "Can you get Malia ready for me?" I ask.

"What's going on? Frankie just told me Reggie's got Ziggy?"

"He'll let him go if I go home," I say, and she gasps. "Please get Malia for me."

"He'll hurt you, Anna."

"And if I don't go back, he might hurt Michelle, or worse, Ziggy. He won't stop until I go back. I don't have a choice. Get Malia and don't tell anyone I've gone."

"Are you sure about this?" she mutters.

"Yes. I'll be fine. I survived this long, didn't I?" I smile. "And you have to stay here with your mum. No one's safe just yet and I don't want anything bad to happen to you two."

Eva nods her head sadly. It isn't like we haven't been here a hundred times before. I hug her and kiss her cheek. "Quick, get Malia."

Once I have everything packed, I head downstairs and go out the back door. There's never anybody out there, and with all the guys currently in church, it means we can leave without being spotted. I take Malia by the hand and head for the gates. There's a large black car with tinted windows waiting, and a man I recognize as one of Reggie's men gets out. He opens the door and we get inside. I strap Malia into the seat. "Why do you look sad, mummy?" she asks, touching my face.

"I'm not sad," I lie.

"Is it because you like it at the club?"

"Maybe," I say. "As long as I'm with you, I don't mind where we are. You make me happy." I smile and she returns it.

We get to Reggie's house and he's outside waiting for me. I step from the car, leaving Malia in her seat. "Where's Ziggy and Michelle?" I ask.

Reggie smirks. "Come inside, Princess. We'll talk." He glances around. The street isn't busy, but he has a lot of rich neighbours. He doesn't like to look like a fool in front of people.

"Not until they get in this car, so I know they're safe." I sound much braver than I feel. Reggie smiles stiffly and stuffs his hands in his pockets. He casually comes down the steps towards me. When he gets close enough, he leans in towards my ear.

"You don't make the rules, Anna. Get inside, now." I feel around behind me and hold onto the door handle of the car. I shake my head and Reggie's jaw goes rigid. He glances around again and then grips the top of my arm tightly. I try to hold onto the door handle, but it's no use. He wrenches me away and drags me up the steps. "Darrell, get Malia out the car," he shouts over his shoulder.

"Let them go," I cry, tripping up one of the steps and hitting my shin hard. Reggie pulls me to my feet and up the last few steps. He gets me through the door and throws me to the floor, and I scramble away from him as he looms over me.

"Get up," he hisses. "Before Malia comes in." I push myself to stand, but I stay pressed against the wall. Darrell carries Malia inside and she immediately reaches for Reggie. She smiles and kisses his cheek, and when her eyes find me, she frowns. I often wondered before I left him if she could sense the danger in the air. "Juliette," he shouts. Malia's nanny comes rushing in. She sees Malia and squeals with delight. I never agreed to Malia having Juliette around. Not only because I was pretty certain that she was fucking Reggie, but also because I wanted to look after my own child. "Please take Malia to her room until I tell you it's okay to come out," he says. She nods and takes Malia by the hand and leads her away.

My Mobile rings and Reggie holds out his hand for it. I pass it to him and he grins when he checks the caller ID. He answers as he takes my hand and pulls me towards his office.

"Riggs. Twice in one day. How privileged." He presses the speaker button and Riggs' curse words fill the silence. "If I could just stop you there," says Reggie calmly. "Anna came of her own free will." He closes his office door, locking it. He places the Mobile on his desk and smiles. "Anna called me to tell me she was ready to come home. Did you upset her?"

"You'd better not have hurt Michelle," Riggs yells. His concern for Michelle over me burns my heart. I give my head a shake. How dare I be jealous of his feelings towards her when she's the mother of his child.

Reggie checks his watch and laughs. "Of course, it's past noon. I didn't get a chance to follow out my threat because my wife came home, and now I have her, well, I guess I won't need to."

"Put Anna on," yells Riggs.

"Let me check she wants to speak with you first," says Reggie, and then he flicks his hand, indicating for me to talk.

"I'm here," I mutter.

"What the hell were you thinking? I was sorting it!" yells Riggs.

"I'm sorry," I begin to cry. Today has been so emotional that it catches up with me hard and I can't stop the tears as they flow. "I was trying to help."

"Did you go back because of what I said?" he growls.

"No, of course not. I wanted him to give Michelle and Ziggy back," I say.

"Why don't you ever just talk to me first? You make these stupid fucking decisions and for what?" he yells. "You cause me more trouble!"

"You never wanted to talk, remember! But won't happen again, will it," I snap. "I'm not your problem anymore. We're over. Done."

"This is all very lovely." Reggie sighs, reaching for me. I resist, but he tugs me hard and I fall against him. "Lovers break-ups are always interesting, especially when they involve my wife. But I'd like to get reacquainted with Anna now, so . . . " His fist hits my stomach and I double over, coughing hard. "We'll discuss the docks in an hour."

"What are you doing to her?" yells Riggs. "Take the docks. Have what the fuck you want and return what's mine."

"Oh, you can have the crack whore and the kid, but Anna is mine," smiles Reggie. He shoves me hard with his foot and I fall onto my side. "An hour." He disconnects the call and then smiles down at me. It's not the nice smile he saves for important business associates. It's not even the same smile he saves for the people he hates. This smile tells me that he wants to hurt me. He wants to hurt me bad.

I swallow two pain killers. My ribs ache. I watch Malia sleeping soundly in her old bed in her old room. She was pleased to see all her toys and spent hours playing while I lay on her bed watching. A shadow creeps up and Reggie peers into Malia's bedroom. "She looks happy to be home," he whispers. "Come and have dinner."

I'm not hungry, but what's the point in telling him that? He'll still force me to eat. I wince with each step and grip my ribs. The pain is making me feel nauseous. I sit at the dining table and one of the house staff brings out the evening meal. "Did you let Ziggy go home?" I ask quietly. I can't stand the thought of Ziggy being distressed.

"That's not your concern. You are home where you belong, and I don't want to hear another word from your mouth about Riggs or anything to do with him."

"I just want to know that Ziggy is okay. He's Malia's friend and . . . "

Reggie grips my hair and tugs my head closer to him, and I wince as pain shoots through me. "Anna, don't push me," he warns.

A tall blond enters the room. She smiles confidently and doesn't seem at all put off by the scene before her. Reggie releases me and stands, greeting the woman with a kiss to each cheek. I've never seen this woman before, but even I have to admit she looks good standing next to my husband. They speak quietly to one another and Reggie gently strokes his thumb down her jawline. It's a gentle move and one I've not seen from him for some time, especially towards me. "Go to bed, Anna," he says dismissively over his shoulder. He takes the woman by her hand and leads her from the room.

I give it a few seconds and then rush after them, peering around the door to see them head upstairs. When they're out of sight, I creep towards the downstairs office. I press my ear to the door and listen for any signs that someone is inside. When I'm confident it's empty, I sneak in, careful to close the door as quietly as I can behind me. I rush over to the telephone and sigh with happiness when I hear the dialling tone. I call Eva because it's the only Mobile number I know by heart. It rings a few times and then she answers.

"Eva, it's me," I say quickly. "Has Riggs got Michelle and Ziggy back?"

"Anna, thank god, you're okay. Where are you? Did he hurt you?" she asks.

There's a rustling sound and Eva curses. Riggs' voice fills the line. "Anna, where are you?"

"That doesn't matter right now. I don't have long. Is Ziggy home?"

"No. Reggie said he'd call with a location, but we're still waiting."

"Okay. He's going to be preoccupied for a short time. I'll look around here and see if I can find them. There's a basement." I reel off the address.

"Are there guards around?" he asks. I move the slats on the blinds and look out the front. There's one guy leaning against the wall outside and I relay that to Riggs. "Something isn't right, Anna. He wouldn't leave you alone to find a phone. He wouldn't risk you just walking out the front door and only leaving one man on guard."

"I have to go." I sigh. "Before he finds me here. Take care, Riggs. I'll do my best to find them for you . . . " I pause. "And I'm sorry, for everything."

"Anna, I didn't mean what I—" he begins, but I disconnect the call. I can't listen to him tell me he's sorry and he'll get me out of here because I can't be strong if I'm waiting around to be rescued. I learned a long time ago that I can only rely on myself.

I get out of the office unseen. The house has three floors plus a basement. If he was going to hide Michelle and Ziggy here, then the basement is where I'd find them.

The door to the basement is locked. I rummage around the kitchen to find a key but come up with nothing. I go back to the office and find a ring of keys in the top drawer of Reggie's desk. There're around ten keys.

Going back to the door, I try each and every one. My hands shake so bad, I almost drop the bunch several times. I get to the last key and hold my breath as I insert it.

The lock clicks open, and I do a silent cheer, but then something hard presses against the back of my head and I freeze.

I close my eyes when the sound of the hammer cocks back and I realize it's a gun. "Well, well, well. You looking for something, sweetheart?" It's a female voice. I swallow the lump in my throat.

"Are you gonna at least let me turn around?" I ask.

"Sure. I'd like to see the look on your face when Reggie comes," she says. I slowly turn around. There's a reason I thought this woman looked good at Reggie's side— she has the same cruel eyes. "Pretty little thing, aren't ya," she mutters. "I can see why the kid's cute."

"Does Reg know you have a gun in the house?" I ask. "He hates weapons around his princess."

She arches her brow. "Oh hunny, haven't you heard? I'm the new princess in town." She smiles confidently. Reggie enters the kitchen and stops suddenly when he sees the gun pointing at me. "I was wondering what kept you," he says. "What's going on?"

"Little miss cute was trying to get in the basement," says the woman.

"I was looking for wine, Reggie. I know you keep all the good stuff locked away and it's my first night home. I should be able to get shit-faced on the good stuff," I snap. "And your mistress here pulls a fucking gun on me."

"Crystal, baby." Reggie sighs. He gently takes her arm and removes the gun from her grasp. "We don't need that."

"Are you just gonna let her creep around the house like that?" she asks.

"You mean my house? Mine and Reggie's?" I cut in. It pains me to even say our names in the same sentence, but half the game is making him believe I want to be here. It's what might keep me alive. "Why did you bring me back here if you've found a replacement?" I ask him. "A cheaper one at that."

Crystal's hand lashes out and she claws at my face. Reggie grips her around the waist and pulls her away from me. I hold my cheek and smile. "Cheap and nasty," I add.

"Enough," yells Reggie, trying hard to control the crazy woman in his arms.

"I want her gone, Reggie," she yells. "Her and that little brat."

"Wow. Are you going to let her badmouth your daughter like that?" I ask. "Can I get the wine or not?"

"No. Stay where you are," he growls, then he drags Crystal from the room. As soon as they leave, I pull the door open and rush down into the Mobilear. It's dark and I feel around for a light.

"Ziggy? Michelle?" I whisper. There's no response. I find a switch and the room is bathed in light. It's empty apart from the racks of wine.

Footsteps hit the steps and I pretend to browse the bottles. Crystal appears, followed by Reggie. She must have gotten free because he looks pissed and she's ready to pounce at me again. I'm not worried— Reggie is only okay if it's his hands on me, but he won't allow someone else to hurt me. He grabs her wrist and tries to pull her away.

"So, am I going or staying?" I ask casually, pulling out a bottle of red and reading the label.

"Going!" she screams.

"Reggie?" I ask.

"I'm in charge," she yells. "Not him." I wince at her words. She's clearly new to Reggie, still in the honeymoon stage of their relationship. I hear his hand connect with her flesh, but I don't watch. Instead, I go back to browsing the wine. Blow after blow reigns on her until she doesn't make a sound. I glance up and she's on her knees, doubled over on the ground. The empathetic person in me wants to go to her, but it'll only make things worse for us both. "Go upstairs and get naked," he growls. I go back to the wine. "Anna," he yells. "I'm talking to you."

Chapter 16

RIGGS

It's been three days since I spoke to Anna. Three days of sitting in this truck, watching Reggie's house, and I still don't have Ziggy home. Men come and go all day long, but I've only seen Reggie once. He stood on his doorstep for seconds like lord of the fuckin' manor before going back inside. A doctor arrived this morning and left after ten minutes. The thought that Reggie's hurt Anna makes me sick.

I dial a number and press the Mobile to my ear. "Reggie," I say coldly. "The docks are open and ready. What am I expecting?"

"Two containers. Unload them into the waiting lorries. Once it's done, Ziggy will be returned to you."

"And Michelle?" I ask.

"Ouch. Not Anna?" he asks, and I realize he probably has me on loudspeaker with Anna nearby.

"You've made it clear that's not going to happen, so . . . "

"You're giving up?" he says. "What if I told you there is a way?"

"I'm listening." I sigh.

"Leave London. If you and your gang leave London, you can have Anna."

"That can't happen," I say firmly. "My club's been here for too long and we worked hard to get our part of London. You want me to give everything, the docks, the businesses? I won't give it up to the mob."

"Oh well, I'll just have to keep her, although I'm not sure how much more she can take. She doesn't have as much stamina these days. Did you find that?" He's goading me.

"Not really, Reggie. Maybe she just doesn't perform for you. With me, she couldn't get enough." I hate talking about her like this, like she's a whore.

The call disconnects and Cree sighs. "Why can't we just put a fucking bullet in him? Blow him up or something?"

"You were the one telling me we can't cause that sort of unrest over a woman and now you want me to blow him up?" I smirk and he laughs. "We'll bide our time. He can't keep her in there forever. Eventually, he has to trust her. Before, when she was in a relationship with him, she said she had a lot of freedom. He never expected her to leave him, so she could come and go as she pleased."

"Yeah, but then she left him. He won't ever trust her again. You wanna sit out here for years waiting?"

I shake my head slowly. The thought of not having Anna for years kills me inside. I have to get her back. The front door opens, and I sit up in my seat, holding my breath. I release it with disappointment when a blond steps out, Reggie following behind her. She stops at the top step and turns to him. "She look beat up to you?" asks Cree, squinting.

"I can't see shit from this far back, but she's definitely got black eyes." I reach for the binoculars off the back seat and take a closer look. "Yeah, brother, she's a mess."

Reggie strokes a hand down her face gently and then his fingers grip her neck. He moves his face closer to hers and speaks with venom, spittle hitting her. She winces and I see fear there. A hand reaches from inside the doorway. There's no mistaking that it's Anna's. I notice her wedding band is back in place. She places her hand gently on his shoulder as if to calm him. He releases the blond and I see her shoulders sag in relief. Anna steps out of the house and he wraps his arms around her and kisses her. I pass the binoculars to Cree. I can't watch that shit because it makes me question how real it is. Cree groans. "Fuck, man, he's practically fucking her on the step," he mutters.

"Thanks for that." I sigh. "I don't need the image painting."

"Relax, you know it's fake. She's in survival mode, and by the looks of things, he's beating up on blondie, which means Anna is stepping up the good wife routine."

I ball my fists. "Yeah, it's what all that entails that bothers me." My Mobile rings. "Chains, what we got brother?" I answer.

"Two containers. All filled with kids' dolls. You want me to take the head off one and see exactly what we got?" he asks.

"Yeah. I need to know what's gonna flood our streets."

There's some rustling. "Coke, Pres. If all these dolls are full, then he's looking at a million easily. Maybe more"

"Right. I'll let the mayor know. Get it loaded into the lorries before they get suspicious. Tail them. I want to know where it ends up."

I disconnect and then dial the mayor. "Finn," he whispers. "I'm in a meeting. Is it urgent?"

"Very. We need to meet now."

"Shit." He sighs. "That's not good if you wanna meet in person. I'll come to you. The Windsor?"

"Yeah. See you in thirty minutes."

When we arrive at The Windsor, Pinky nods her head towards the back room. We find the mayor looking angsty and uncomfortable surrounded by bodyguards. We step into the room and they move back to the corners. "Mayor," I say, shaking his hand.

"Make it quick, Finn. I've got a busy day."

"We're a few hours away from two containers full of cocaine hitting the streets of London. I don't know anything about it, if it's good or bad, where it's come from."

He glares at me and the blood vessel in his forehead threatens to burst. "Continue," he mutters carefully.

"Reggie Miller is behind it. I've lost control over the docks and he's using my men to unload it." The words feel bitter on my tongue. "He wants to bring in more in a matter of days."

The mayor slams his hands on the table and stands. "Are you fucking kidding me? How am I only hearing about this now?"

"I was trying to get it under control."

"Well, you clearly fucked that up. How the hell did he get control of the docks?" He begins to pace.

"He took my son and my ex. They were at the park and he took them."

"So you gave him the docks?" he yells.

"What the fuck was I supposed to do? It's a temporary arrangement until I can come up with something better."

The mayor leans forward across the table until he's inches away from me. "You were supposed to let him have the kid and the ex and keep control of my FUCKING DOCKS!" he yells.

I stand up and my chair scrapes the hard floor. The bodyguards move closer, sensing my fraying temper. "I'll sort it out," I say through gritted teeth.

"Damn right, you will. You've risked the lives of hundreds. He'll have half of London hooked on his shit because I can bet my life it's better than what we allow out there." He's right. What we put on the streets is not as strong as what can be gotten in some places. Our rules are strict. It's expensive, not as strong, and we control exactly how much we allow out there. Reggie will make it stronger, cheaper, and easier to obtain, meaning the streets will be flooded. Crime will go up and the mayor will look like he's lost control of London.

"I've got the lorries being tailed. I'll let you know where it ends up."

"I'll have the police force on standby," he mutters, pulling out his Mobile.

"You can't raid it until I get my boy back," I say firmly.

He laughs, it's cold and bitter. "The fuck I can't. You want me to risk the streets for one kid? We'll be saving thousands more."

He puts the call into the Chief of Police, and I glance at Cree. I won't be giving up the location until my boy is back safe.

We leave The Windsor just as my Mobile lights up. "Pres," says Chains. "A packaging warehouse. It's full of workers, but these boxes have been delivered around the back. I don't think the workers know about the secret business out back. I think it's the same kind of set-up Marshall has."

"Right. Text me the address and get out of there. The Met will be all over it as soon as I have Ziggy."

Next, I call Reggie. "Where's my kid?" I growl. I'm done with the fucking about. I'm close to doing exactly what Cree said.

"Your men did a good job today. I'll require the same service tomorrow."

"Fine, just give me Ziggy and Michelle," I growl.

"Tonight. I'll send you the address. But Riggs, it's a black-tie event, so don't show up in club kuttes."

Bonnie slips a dagger into the garter of her stockings. "You sure about this?" she asks. "Won't Anna get the wrong impression?"

"I need Reggie to think I'm over Anna." I tuck a gun in my holster under my arm.

"I think we'll be checked for weapons," she says.

"I know the security at the event. It's on mutual ground, so Reggie will most likely be tooled up too."

Chains straightens up his jacket. Leia watches him and I frown. Maybe having them go together wasn't a good idea, but mum convinced me. Leia's got a good aim, so she'll be worth having with us. I just wish it wasn't on Chains' arm.

Cree loads the van with guns. The plan is he'll be outside with the rest of my men, just in case it all goes wrong.

We arrive at the Mayfair Hotel in central London. The charity event tonight is for victims of drug abuse. The irony.

Most guests go through the body scanner. The head of security ushers us around with a wink. Bonnie hooks her arm through my own. "I hate shit like this," she utters. "A bunch of rich asses pretending to give a crap about the charity. It's an excuse to wave cash around and drink champagne."

"I've got to get Ziggy and then we can leave."

"You really think it'll be that simple?" she asks. I shake my head.

We stay by the bar, giving me the perfect view of the entrance. After an hour, there's still no sign of Reggie, and I'm beginning to get impatient. I head to the bathroom, and as I'm passing the female door, Anna steps out, almost running into me. I push her back into the bathroom so fast that she gasps. There are two other women in there who look surprised to see a six-foot male in their bathroom. "Get out," I hiss. They don't wait around to be asked twice.

My lips crash against Anna's before the door closes. I feel around for the lock, clicking it into place. I rub my hands over her waist, along her ass, and pull her flush against me. "Fuck," I pant against her lips. She wriggles against me and I realize she's pushing me away. I grip her wrists and hold her still. "Don't fucking push me away," I growl.

"He'll come looking for me," she hisses.

"Then let him find me balls deep inside you," I snap, lifting her onto the sink unit and stepping between her legs. She hits my chest hard in protest. "You fucking him, Anna?" I growl and she stills, avoiding eye contact. "Are you with him? Like for real?" I ask. She shakes her head but still won't meet my eyes. "Anna," I hiss.

"What do you want me to say, Riggs? I stepped back into the lion's den and now I'm paying the price. I have to play along or he'll kill me. Do you know what the thought of leaving Malia alone with that monster does to me?" she cries. "He's changed, and not for the better. If I was you, I'd leave London like he wants because he won't stop."

"Until he's dead," I say, and she laughs sarcastically. "You think he's invincible?" I ask.

"I think he's dangerous. I've spent days watching him torture a woman who I think deep down, he loves. He makes her watch us." A choked cry leaves her throat and she sucks in a deep, shaky breath. "She sobs because she loves him too, but he's fighting it. He's scared to love her in case it makes him weak like you."

"Like me?" I repeat.

"Love is what will bring you to your knees. That's what he keeps saying. Your love for Ziggy. Your love for Michelle."

"My love for you," I mutter, stroking my thumb down her cheek.

"No," she snaps, pushing my hand away. "You don't love me. Get Ziggy and Michelle back and then leave London. None of this is as important as them. You can move your club anywhere."

I step back, confused by her behaviour. "I'm not leaving London. I'm not giving him what he wants."

Anna jumps down from the sink unit and straightens her black silk dress. "Then you're stupid. I'm doing what I have to, to survive. You need to do the same." She heads for the door.

"I'm coming for you, Anna. You and Malia."

She pauses with her back to me and her hand on the door. "I don't want you to, Finn. We've said too much, you've said too much, and you hurt me." My name on her lips makes me shudder. She continues. "Ziggy will be returned to you tonight. Michelle is still locked up somewhere. He's using her to push you out. Keep everyone close. He's still watching the club and he'll take anyone he can use to win this war."

"What if I was to take you," I mutter, moving behind her and wrapping my hand gently around her throat. "Right now," I whisper into her ear.

"Then he'd kill Ziggy. He realized quickly that our bond wasn't enough to get you to leave London. That's why I have to play along. If I'm no use to him, he'll kill me."

"Tell him the warehouse is being watched by the cops. It'll gain his trust. Wait until I have Ziggy back before you tell him."

She glances over her shoulder at me. "You need his trust." I run my hand along her collarbone and down her chest. She closes her eyes and I know she feels my erection pressing against her ass. I slip my hand into her dress and into her bra, and she hisses. "This is for emergencies," I whisper, leaving a small Mobile phone in her bra. "It's small enough to hide anywhere. And just for the record, I'm sorry for what I said. I was pissed. But I meant what I said about you being mine, Anna. No words, no argument can break that. So, I'll be coming for you and then I'll make you listen to me properly." I unlock the door and step out of view as she rushes out.

I re-join Chains and the women. "Everything okay?" he asks.

"I saw Anna," I whisper in a low voice so only he can hear me. "Ziggy will be returned tonight. I gave her information about the cops raiding the warehouse," I add.

His eyes almost bug out of his head. "Fuck, Riggs, are you thinking straight?"

"Are you questioning me?" I ask, raising my brow. He shakes his head. "Good. She needs to build trust with him. The mayor will need to find another way to bring him down."

Reggie glides towards me with Anna on his arm. He gives a smug smile. "Good evening, boys," he says.

"Where's Ziggy?" I snap. "We did what you asked."

"Follow me," he says and smiles. His hand slips down to Anna's ass as they lead us outside. He takes us out into the parking lot, where there's a black minivan with dark windows waiting by the entrance. "There's a further shipment coming in tomorrow. Let me know when it's clear for the boat to dock," says Reggie. He taps the side of the van and the driver steps out.

"Too much traffic at the docks will attract attention. It can't be a daily drop-off point," I say.

"You'll make it work," says Reggie firmly.

"Just give me my kid," I growl. The driver opens up the side door to Ziggy lying lifeless on a mattress. Anna gasps and covers her mouth. "What the fuck is wrong with him?" I yell, moving to the van. Reggie pulls out a gun and points it at my head. I freeze.

"Do we have a deal, Riggs?" asks Reggie.

"Reg, please. Stop this," whispers Anna, glancing around nervously.

Reggie grins at her. "What did you say to me?" There's a dangerous edge to his voice. "Are you defending this piece of shit?" he asks, clicking the safety clip of the gun.

I press my head against the gun and stare hard into Reggie's eyes. "Do it," I growl. "Let's see how you get your shit into the docks without me."

He smiles with ease, then pulls Anna into his side and turns the gun on her. She closes her eyes and grips the hand that holds her tightly. "Maybe I need to start pulling the trigger on the people you love," he says.

I shrug my shoulders. "I don't want her now she's fucked you. I'm bored with these games, Reggie. I'll bring your goods in tomorrow, but if it alerts the cops, that's on you, I've tried to warn you."

Reggie shoves Anna away from him and she stumbles and falls to the ground. I ball my fists, desperate to beat the shit out of him and to scoop Anna up from the ground. Instead, I reach into the van and gather up my son. He doesn't stir but he's breathing.

NICOLA JANE

Chapter 17

ANNA

We arrive home and I go straight upstairs to check on Malia. She's sleeping soundly. I remove the small Mobile from my bra and hide it deep in Malia's wardrobe. Reggie never comes in here, so it should be safe. I move to the bathroom to wash up the cuts to my hands and knee, which I grazed when I fell.

"Get undressed," mutters Reggie as he steps into the bathroom behind me. I glare at him through the mirror.

"You pointed a gun at my head," I snap.

"You should be thankful I didn't pull the trigger," he quips.

"Where's Michelle?" I ask coldly. "Why didn't you give her back to Riggs?"

"Michelle is enjoying her stay. She's earning her keep well and is proving popular with my customers."

"What are you talking about?"

He pulls his Mobile from his pocket and holds it out to me. I watch the screen as a video recording begins to play. I recognize Michelle, naked and laughing as she leans over a table and snorts a line of white powder. A man snakes a hand around her throat and licks her face. Another man slaps her across the face, then she opens her mouth as he stuffs his cock into it. I pass the Mobile back, unable to watch any more.

"She isn't in her right mind. You can't get her high on drugs and then say she's enjoying that. She's too high to make a choice."

"I don't give a fuck if she's consenting or not, Anna. Neither do they. She's a crackhead. She gets what she needs and she pays for it. I gave her a choice— she could go home with Ziggy or stay at the whorehouse and work for me. Guess what she chose."

"That's unfair," I sob. "Of course, she'd choose drugs, she's an addict. You preyed on her weakness."

Reggie rolls his eyes and loosens his tie. "Enough of the dramatics. Get naked." I ignore his request, and instead, I stare at him blankly through the mirror. The sex doesn't bother me. I willingly slept with him for many years. We're married, so I don't feel violated even though I don't want to have sex with him. But he's got peculiar tastes, tastes that he acquired later in our marriage.

He smirks, probably delighting in my lack of response. He grips the silk dress at the shoulders and tugs it down my body. I stare at myself in the mirror. Bite marks cover my breasts and stomach. Bruises where he's restrained my ankles and wrists too tightly are visible.

"Gorgeous," he whispers to himself. He turns me to face him, pushing me against the washbasin. He sucks a nipple into his mouth as he unfastens his shirt, and as he shrugs out of it, he bites the soft skin of my breast hard. I hiss and grip the unit behind me. He smiles, his eyes alight with lust. He sinks to his knees and runs his hand down my leg before gently kissing my inner thigh. I grip the unit again when he sinks his teeth there and sucks hard enough to draw blood. He leans back to admire his handy work and I wonder for the hundredth time what possible pleasure he gets out of this. He pushes his face between my legs, and I scream out loud when his teeth scrape against my sensitive area.

I manage a few hours of unsettled sleep. Reggie didn't ease up for hours last night and my body is feeling the after-effects of that as I stretch out. The bedroom door opens, and Crystal comes in carrying a tray full of breakfast. Reggie's new cruel thing is to have her serve me. She avoids my eye and places the tray on the bedside table. "Crystal," I whisper. "Please stay and eat."

She shakes her head. "He'll never know. He'll be in his office now for hours." She stares longingly at the croissant. "Please," I beg. I hold it out and she takes it carefully. "I don't know why Reggie is doing this to you," I say.

"Because you're back," she mutters.

"But he doesn't want me. I don't get it."

"He's obsessed with you," she adds. "He told me that. He needs you nearby, and he doesn't know why, but he can't be without you."

"That makes no sense," I mutter. "He treats me like crap. How did you end up here?" I ask.

"We met in one of his clubs." She shrugs, nibbling at the pastry. "I fell for him."

"Even after everything he's done these last few days?" I ask, and she nods her head. I feel like I'm looking at my eighteen-year-old self. I was infatuated with Reggie and how powerful he seemed to be. No one could touch me with Reggie by my side. "There are other men out there who will protect you and not treat you badly," I sigh. "Reggie will never treat you good."

"You're wrong," she mumbles. "He did before you came back. He's testing my loyalty. We'll get back to how we were," she nods.

"Breakfast for two?" comes Reggie's voice and Crystal drops the croissant to the floor and spins to face him. He lingers in the doorway, looking back and forth between us.

"She was helping me eat," I say. "My arms hurt."

"Is that true, Crystal?" he asks.

She shakes her head. "Sorry," she mumbles.

"You're hungry?" he asks, and she nods. "Why didn't you just say?" he asks. He steps into the room and closes the door.

"I have to sort Malia," I mutter, not liking the uneasy feeling spreading through the room. I throw my legs over the side of the bed.

He points a finger at me as he saunters towards Crystal. "Stay," he growls. I grit my teeth, knowing whatever he's about to do will be cruel. He wraps his hand into her hair and pushes her to her knees while he unfastens his trousers.

"Please, Reggie," I groan. "I can't watch this." I cover my face with my hands.

"If you don't, then I'll make it worse for her," he says. He wants to humiliate her and make her feel worthless. "Every protest, every sob, and I'll make it worse. Am I clear?" he asks. I nod my head.

Crystal takes his cock eagerly and I hold back my tears. She's so in love with him that she'll do anything to be close to him. He fucks her mouth so hard that she gags several times. Tears stream from her eyes and as he gets closer to release, he chokes her until she passes out and then slaps her to bring her around. I clench my fists so hard, my nails cut into my palms. I want so badly to stab him and to make it all stop. When he finally releases into her mouth, it's with such force that she chokes. He places his hand over her mouth, forcing her to swallow. He pulls her to her feet and brings her face close to his. "Next time you are hungry, you come to me. Understand?" She nods her head and he shoves her away from him. "Get out of my sight."

"Why are you treating her so badly when I know you love her?" I ask bitterly once Crystal's left the room.

He laughs. "I don't love anyone. She shouldn't have put a gun to your head. Only I am allowed to do that. She thought she could make rules up around here."

"So you thought you'd put her in her place?"

"Get dressed. We have some business to attend to," he says. I stand and let the sheets fall away from my bruised body. His eyes run over me.

"If a man did this to Malia, would you be angry?" I ask.

His face turns stony. "Get dressed, Anna."

"Would you want this for her?"

Reggie leaves the room, slamming the door behind him. I smile at my small victory. Despite his cruel behaviour, he loves Malia very much, and I'm sure he'd kill any man who treated her like he treats women.

The car stops outside a warehouse. "Why am I here?" I ask.

"Because I don't trust you to stay home."

"I could just as easily run from here," I point out.

"And leave Malia?" He smirks because he's right. I could never run unless she was with me, and he's doing a good job of making sure we're never out of the house together.

I follow him through a packing warehouse and realize I never passed on the information to Reggie about the police. I glance behind me at the entrance. Nothing seems out of place. "You package toys?" I ask as women all around me stuff dolls into boxes.

"Something like that," he says.

He pulls a plastic sheet back for me to step through and we're at the back of the warehouse, where two long tables run down the room, women in underwear standing on either side, spooning white powder onto weighing scales. Men dressed in black and holding guns are positioned down both sides of the room and at the entrances. "Shit," I hiss. Reggie smirks.

"Sit there," he tells me, pointing to a stool. I sit and he turns to a man holding a gun. "If she moves from that seat, shoot her in the leg." The man nods once, and Reggie heads off towards an office at the back of the room.

I watch the women packing the drugs like it's nothing, like what they're handling won't destroy lives. Reggie is gone for at least half an hour. My ass is numb and I'm relieved when I see him coming towards me. "Onto the next thing on my list," he says, and I groan. This is going to be a long day.

I wince at the sound of a fist hitting flesh. I close my eyes and picture my life before all of this, even before I ran from Reggie. Yes, he was controlling, and yes, he beat me, but at least I had some freedom. In the daytimes when he was working, my life was easy, and I never witnessed anything like this.

A man hangs on a meat hook, his hands cuffed. His head is lolling to one side and both eyes are swollen shut. His top half is naked, and bruises are appearing in front of my eyes. Reggie wipes his hands on a piece of cloth and throws it beside my feet. "Finish him off," he pants to the two men standing nearby. I pick up the cloth and stuff it in my bag, then follow Reggie from the warehouse.

"What did he do?" I ask.

"Marshall Ankers is a scumbag," he says through gritted teeth. "Running back and forth between two men at war." He gives me an annoyed look as we climb into the car. "Why do you care anyway?" he snaps.

"I don't," I shrug. "Just wondered."

Next, we go to what Reggie refers to as 'the club'. On the outside, the building is covered in graffiti and looks abandoned. It's not the sort of place you'd stumble across because the buildings all around it are empty and derelict.

He pushes through a metal door and we go down some stairs. He knocks three times on the door at the bottom and someone looks through a peephole on the other side of the door. It opens and Reggie shakes hands with a huge man dressed all in black.

It's two in the afternoon and the place is busy. It smells of sex and alcohol and a low beat pumps out in the background. The lighting is dim, which gives it a dirty feel. There are some couches near the bar area where five women are lounging in underwear. None of them are engaging in conversation, just staring around the club idly. They look unkempt and in need of a good wash.

One girl eyes us as we pass by. Her hair is scraggly, and her black mascara is smudged under her eyes.

An important-looking man approaches us and shakes Reggie's hand. Reggie hands him a taped-up package. It's the same as what the women were packing at the warehouse. "Thanks, man. Your girl is working hard today." He smiles. "I told her about the new delivery, and she's been working that ass since."

I look to where the man points and find Michelle is naked and straddling a fat, old man. My heart breaks all over again. For her, for Ziggy, and for Riggs, because he's tried so hard to help her.

"Good. Give her enough to keep her ass working here for years. I've had a lot of interest in her," says Reggie.

"Probably because she looks good at the minute. Once she's taken this shit for a month, she'll look like all the rest," says the man.

Reggie pulls out his Mobile and presses record. He points it to Michelle as she bounces on the old man. He records for about thirty seconds, then cuts it off. "A present for your biker boyfriend," he says to me before stuffing his mobile back in his pocket.

By the time we get home, Malia is having her dinner. She smiles at me happily and I hate that I've hardly seen her for the last few days. "Can we watch a movie, daddy?" she asks.

"Sure," he mutters distractedly, staring down at his Mobile phone. "Go choose one and I'll be in soon." We decide on *Moana* because I know Reggie won't join us.

Chapter 18

RIGGS

I stare down at my mobile. The video of Michelle screwing some fat, old bastard plays out. I'd had the same sort of recording last night, only she was snorting cocaine. Cree looks over my shoulder. "That's Reggie's whore club."

"Get the guys together. We need to make a move tonight."

"Just like that? You want to go right in?"

"I'm tired of waiting. If this is his club, it's where Michelle is at. We're gonna take her back."

An hour later, I play the video for my brothers. "We go in tonight. I want this place burnt to the ground," I say.

"I have a connection that can take these women and put them up in a hostel. There are key workers there who can help the women get off the drugs and back into society," says Cree.

I smile gratefully. "The plan is, we get the girls out, we kill any of Reggie's men who try to stop us, then we burn it," I add.

"The thing is, we have to get over the tracks unseen," says Chains. He holds up a bunch of football shirts. "And it just so happens that Chelsea Football Club is playing tonight. So, we scrap the kuttes and pretend to be on a lads' boozy night out to watch the match." There are a few groans around the table, but that's more to do with the choice of football club than anything else.

"Who will stay behind to watch the families?" asks Rock.

"You," I say, and he laughs knowingly. Rock is a man mountain and I know he can handle anything back here at the club.

We step out into the club parking lot. Two minibuses await us and we load up. We look ridiculous donning our football shirts and mum insisted on a group photo for the club wall of fame.

It's not long before we arrive across the tracks and to Reggie's dingy sex club. Cree fills us in on the way after speaking to a contact. Apparently, Reggie hooks the girls on his drugs, getting them into debt, then the only way to pay it off is to work here.

I shudder at the thought of what the poor women are going through inside. The place is a dump. We gather around Cree, who goes through the layout briefly. Then he leads us towards the metal door and down some steps. He knocks three times and the door opens slightly. "There's about fifteen of us," says Cree to the bouncer. "We have cash." He smiles, waving a bunch of notes. The door opens wider.

"I need some identification," growls the bouncer. "We take a copy off every guest."

"Sure, no problem," says Cree. He reaches into his pocket and then pulls his fist out fast, connecting hard with the bouncer's face. He stumbles backward and Cree hits him again. I lead the way inside, and as more security comes forward, fights begin to break out. Women scream and rush for the door. We left two of the brothers upstairs to lead the women to safety.

I push my way through the women running and the brothers who are fighting until I spot Michelle. She's passed out on a table and three men are lining up, waiting for the man currently fucking her to finish. Rage fills me and I punch the first guy in the head. He falls to the ground and the second turns to see what the fuss is. He sees me and holds his hands up. "I don't want no trouble," he says.

"Then get out of here," I yell. He scuttles off like the dirtbag he is, followed closely by the third guy.

"Wait your fucking turn," shouts the man fucking her.

"She's passed out," I yell.

"She's warm. I don't give a crap if she's passed out," he snaps.

I pull him away from her and throw him to the floor. He yells at me, but I don't hear shit. I gently tap Michelle on the face. "Baby," I whisper. "Wake up." I feel for a pulse, but it's very weak. I shrug out of the football shirt and put it on Michelle. I scoop her up in my arms and make my way back through the building. "Burn this shit to the ground," I order.

I stand by Michelle's bed, watching her chest move up and down. A small part of me wishes I could love her like I used to. Maybe that would be enough for her to stay clean. But deep down, I don't trust her, and I can't put Ziggy through it all again. Cree got the other women to safety. The Women's Aid shelter made sure they had workers on standby to help the women with the drug problem. It's a long road for all of them, but for the ones who want that help, Cree made it happen. I insisted on bringing Michelle back to the club, where a doctor met us.

He squeezes a bag of fluids into her drip. "She's severely dehydrated. We need to get this into her as fast as possible. Do you have an ETA on a nurse?" he asks. He came straight from the hospital and he's on call, so he's anxious to get back.

Leia pops her head around the door. "You wanted me?" she asks.

"Just in time. You're wanting to be a nurse, right?" I ask.

"Erm, yeah, but I haven't done enough to take over here unsupervised," she says.

"It's fine. It's basic care," says the doctor, then he launches into a speech of what she needs to watch for and how to contact him.

I find Cree in the main room drinking a bourbon. "We did good tonight," he says.

"I know. Just feel like now we've begun, we need to hit the next target quickly."

"Well, this would have all been done earlier if you'd have told the mayor about the warehouse," he points out.

"Anna was there today. I couldn't call it in with her in the building," I repeat.

"And we still don't know why she hasn't told him about the cops watching that place. If he knew, he'd have moved that shit out by now."

I nod. I'd been thinking the same thing. She sounded like she needed desperately to build trust with him. "Maybe she was hoping he'd get caught?"

"She knows he would have walked out of the police station within a day. We need to be careful that she isn't siding with him. Maybe she's falling for him?"

I ball my fists. "That makes no sense. She would have told him about the cops to save his ass. I don't know what's going on there. Maybe she's scared. He'd want to know how she knew, so maybe it just wasn't worth telling him."

I go to my office and pick up the phone. I have the mayor on speed dial. "I've been waiting to hear from you," he snaps.

"Things were complicated. I'm going to text you the address of the warehouse. There are women inside packing the drugs. It's at the back of the warehouse. You have to hit it tonight because during the day there's a whole workforce packaging toys. Too many innocents."

"Did you get your kid back?" he asks.

"Yeah."

"We have someone inside," he says quietly. "Living in the house."

My body goes on alert. "What?"

"I spoke with the Chief of Police yesterday. She's been undercover for a few months, but things are getting worse. She's not sure if she can stick it out. I'm meeting the chief tomorrow, so I'll get more information then, but we're hoping to get to him this way. It's the first time we've ever managed to infiltrate into his life."

"My ex is there," I blurt out. "In the house. She mentioned another woman."

"Well, if you have contact with her, don't tell her about this. You can't blow the officer's cover. We'll hit the warehouse tonight."

He disconnects the call and I quickly send him the address. I begin to feel hope. Maybe we can end Reggie, breaking down his businesses one by one until he has nothing.

I sleep in the chair by Michelle's bed. She's improving hour by hour, and when I wake in the morning, she's staring at me. "Why am I here?" she asks coldly.

"Are you fucking kidding me?" I ask, my voice croaky from sleep. "I found you unconscious being fucked by some man who had teeth missing. There were three more waiting for a turn."

"So what?" she snaps. "It was my choice."

"It was the drug's choice," I mutter. "Get clean. If you want to go back to that kind of thing after, then that's your choice, but right now, the drugs are controlling you."

"I saw Anna. She's always by his side, ya know. Everyone says they're together again."

"Stop," I snap. "You're lucky I haven't put a bullet in you. Do you realize what you did? I had to give up the docks to get my kid back. The kid you took out when I told you not to leave this place. You could have gotten him killed as well as yourself."

"You may as well put a bullet in me. Bringing me back here is like torture."

"Ziggy can't sleep. The doctor has to medicate him, and he lays with me or Frankie all night. He's hardly speaking. I could strangle you," I hiss. "And you wake up from your drug-filled fucking and you don't even ask me how he is? Did you even think about him at all?"

"Of course, I did," she mutters.

"Until they gave you a hit!" I state angrily. "You're staying in this room until you're clean. Cold turkey," I say, and she cries out. "That's the punishment for what you did. I hope every day hurts. Then when you're well again, I'm sending you to Scotland. I want you far away from me and Ziggy, where you can't hurt us anymore."

"Scotland?" she screeches.

"Yes. I have a friend there waiting with a room to rent and a job. You *will* get your life sorted."

"Riggs to the damn rescue," she mutters.

"Call me a fucking saint." I sigh, then I leave, locking her in the room.

My mobile rings and I head for the office as I answer.

"Riggs?" It's Anna and I sigh in relief.

"You okay?" I ask.

"I just called to find out if Ziggy is okay."

I smile. She's putting herself in danger to call me and ask about Ziggy when his own mother doesn't give a crap. "He's okay. A little traumatised, as you can imagine."

"Good. I'm so glad. Reggie's real mad," she whispers. "He just found out about the club. Was that you?" Cree's doubt haunts my brain and I withhold my answer.

"Are you okay?" I repeat.

"Yes. Please be careful. He's screaming into his Mobile in his office. I don't know what he'll do next."

"Tell me about the woman you mentioned before," I say.

"Crystal?" she asks. "She met Reggie and fell in love. She said before I came home, he was good to her. Now, he's awful. He abuses her, hits her, makes her serve me food."

"Anna, can I trust you?"

"Of course, you can," she cries. "Why are you asking me that?"

I push Cree's doubts to one side. "That woman is an undercover cop," I say. Anna falls silent. "Are you there?"

"Yes. She's a cop? What the hell?"

"You can't fuck up and blow her cover. It's very important, Anna."

"But he's raping her. He's doing awful things to her. Why doesn't she leave or get her boss to get her out?"

"They need something on him. You have to help her. Tell her whatever you know. The quicker you help her, the quicker you can get away."

"I have a towel," she says. "I kept it because it has DNA on it. He beat a man . . . " She pauses. "Marshall something."

"Ankers? Is he dead?" That would explain why I haven't heard from him.

"I think so. He told the men who watched to end him. He wiped his hands on the towel."

"Give it to her. I'm not sure it's enough to get anything big on him, but it might help with the bigger picture."

"Anna!" I hear Reggie yelling. "Anna!"

"Coming," she answers. "I have to go. I love you, Riggs." Then she's gone. It's the first time she's said the words to me since all of this happened. I stare at the Mobile in my hand for some time after she's hung up, absorbing the things she said. The thought that she's forgiven me for the things I said gives me hope, and I smile.

Cree sticks his head in the office and then waves a bottle of bourbon and two glasses at me. "I got us front row seats to the drug raid," he says, placing the bottle on my desk. He opens up my laptop and presses a few buttons. "I know this nerd who hacked into the police body cams or some shit. Look," he turns the screen towards me, and we see the live feed off one of the cops' bodycam. They're in a van, assumingly on their way to Reggie's factory.

"Anna called," I say. "She said Reggie's losing his mind over the club." I smile. "She's got a towel with DNA on it. Said she watched Reggie kill Marshall Ankers."

Cree stops mid-pour. "Marshall's dead? Explains why he hasn't been in touch."

"Yeah. He's obviously not been found yet or the mayor would have known."

Cree sits down and pushes a glass towards me. "So, now we need a new supplier? We don't know who Marshall was using."

"Last thing on my mind, brother." I sigh. "Let's get Reggie out of the way first."

"And get Anna back to you," he grins.

"I need her, man. This time without her has shown me just how much I fucking need her."

He nods in understanding. "Eva is missing her and Malia so badly."

"Yeah?" I ask. "You been talking to Eva?"

"Not really." He laughs. "I've been grunting at her and mainly listening. I'm good at listening."

I laugh and shake my head. "Any man can listen. She needs a man who talks to her, Cree. She won't stay around forever. She already asked me when she can go back home, said she doesn't feel right being here without Anna." Cree sits up straighter in his chair, looking alarmed. "Don't worry. I told her she's staying put, her and her mum." He visibly relaxes. "But I can't keep her here forever. She thinks you're not interested in her like that."

"I just can't get my words out around her." He sighs. "It's a fucking joke. I can slit a man's throat for running his mouth off, but I can't talk to a girl I like."

The bodycam shows the officers getting out of the van and all moving towards the factory. Suddenly, there's shouting and yelling as they run through the building, taking the drug workers by surprise. I sit back and take it all in with a satisfied smile on my face. The cops detain the women and the few men who were standing guard. We watch in silence, absorbing every detail with satisfaction.

Almost an hour later, they are still loading up the drugs into evidence bags. Reggie would have flooded the streets with this crap, and he wouldn't have been able to control it or the violence and crime it would have produced.

The mayor calls me. "It's done" is all he says before disconnecting. I don't get a chance to tell him that I already know.

Screams ring out and I sit up alarmed in my bed. It takes me a few seconds to realize it's Michelle that I can hear yelling and crying. I scrub my face with my hands and groan. It's six in the morning. I tuck the sheets around my sleeping boy, thankful that she hasn't woken him. I pad downstairs to her bedroom. The floor below mine is occupied by most of the brothers, so I'm guessing she's woken just about everyone. I unlock the door and Michelle rushes towards me to try and escape. I catch her in time and pull her into my chest. She's sweating and shaking and beating her clenched fists against my chest. "It's okay," I whisper. "You're okay."

Eventually, she relaxes against me and sobs quietly. I slide down the door with her and she scrunches up into my lap. We sit like that for some time until her sobbing subsides.

"I can't do this," she whispers. "I feel like I'm dying."

"You're not dying. You're gonna be just fine. We're running tests on that shit you took to make sure it's pure," I say. Sometimes, dealers will add all kinds of toxins to fill out the product or make it more addictive. "The first few days are always the worst, but it will get easier."

"Few days!" she screeches. "I can't do this for a few days. I want to claw my own fucking skin off."

"Darlin', you don't have a choice. I can't send you to Scotland like this, and I can't send you back out on the streets. You're the mother of my son. I have a responsibility so that when Ziggy is old enough to ask me about you, I can tell him I did right by you."

"Well, isn't that just sweet," she grumbles, getting up off my lap. "But meanwhile, I've got to feel like this?"

I stand. "Yup. Get a shower, it might help, and to be honest, you look a mess."

"You think I give a shit about that right now when my body hurts this bad? Why have you always got to be the fucking saint? The hero of the hour," she spits. "It's okay to just let me go, Riggs. You can tell Ziggy that you tried but I wanted the drugs more, because I do. I want the drugs more than you. More than him." She begins to cry. "I just want one more hit. I need to stop this pain." I shake my head and she tries to slap me across the face but misses. I catch her wrist and haul her ass towards me.

"You won't get another chance to do that," I growl. "I'm trying my goddamn best to do right by you, but bitch, you make it damn near impossible. We're gonna shower now."

I pull her towards the en-suite while she tugs to try and free herself. I turn the shower on and the bathroom begins to fill with steam. Kicking and screaming, I haul her over my shoulder and stand under the spray of water. It soaks into my clothes and my shirt sticks to me.

"Okay," she cries angrily. "I'll shower myself." I lower her to her feet, and she runs her hands over my wet shirt. "You wanna stay?" she whispers. "Remember the times we showered together? Any chance you got to have me wet, you'd take it."

"Stop," I mutter.

"I bet we conceived Ziggy in the shower." She smiles, beginning to pop the buttons on my shirt. "I'll do whatever you want if you give me one last hit." It's like a bucket of ice is thrown over me. I still her hands, then step out of the shower and grab a towel. "Oh, come on, Riggs," she groans.

"Get showered," I mutter, slamming the bathroom door closed behind me.

Chapter 19

ANNA

I place the bowl of cereal in front of Malia, all the while keeping an eye on the door. Reggie just received a call and he's in the hallway yelling into his Mobile about cops. "Daddy sounds cross," says Malia warily. I stroke my hand over her wild bed hair and smile softly. I don't bother to find words of comfort because from the sound of Reggie yelling, I can't deny that he's cross.

I move closer to the door to listen. "You shouldn't listen in, he might catch you," says Crystal as she enters the room.

"Any idea what's wrong?" I ask, and she shakes her head. "No intel from your boss?" I add, and she stops and turns to me. "It's okay, Reggie doesn't know you're undercover." She snatches my wrist and drags me out the back door and into the garden. "Hey," I hiss, pulling my wrist away and rubbing it. Gone is the weak and wounded victim she's been playing these last few days, and in her place stands a stony-faced, angry woman.

"How the fuck do you know?" she hisses.

"Does it matter? Reggie doesn't know. It's not common knowledge."

"Of course, it matters, if my cover gets blown. How many people know?" she snaps.

I shrug. "Maybe I can help you," I suggest, and she rolls her eyes.

"Well, he's hardly confessing all to you, is he?" I snap. "I have a towel with his DNA on it. He ordered a kill on a guy called Marshall."

"And you watched that, did you?" she asks sarcastically.

"Well, no," I stammer. "Not exactly. He beat him though, I saw that part, and then ordered the kill as we left."

"So he told someone to kill Marshall? He used those words?" she asks sceptically.

"Again, no," I say, and she laughs, shaking her head like she thinks I'm pathetic. "He said to finish him off."

"That means fuck all. It could mean wank him for all the judge will care. Finishing someone off means all kinds of things and Reggie isn't stupid. He'll say anything to get off a murder charge, and unless he slit the guy's throat at your feet, we have nothing."

"I went to a warehouse with him. There were drugs there, loads of drugs, and women packing them up."

"The warehouse has been hit by police already. You're too late with that information."

"What about what he's been doing to you?" I ask tentatively. "Can't he get into trouble for rape or something?"

She glares at me like I've just killed her puppy. "No one can know about any of that. If my boss knows how deep undercover I've gone, he'll pull me from the case," she snaps.

"Oh," I mutter.

"Tell me you haven't told anyone that," she growls. I shake my head innocently and swallow hard. I'm pretty sure Riggs won't tell anyone what I said anyway.

She takes a deep breath and releases it slowly. "Look, if he gets arrested for the warehouse, then maybe we could use you as a witness to place him there, but I doubt it will be enough. Reggie is clever, so he will have a way to disassociate himself with the warehouse. We need more. We need much more."

"What about the videos on his phone of the girls he's forcing into prostituting themselves for his drugs?" I ask.

"Who's to say they're his drugs? Who's to say they're being forced? It won't stand up in a court of law. His lawyer will say he's within his rights to visit a whorehouse. Damn, the judge probably goes there with him."

Reggie marches out into the garden, and without thinking, I slap Crystal across the face. "How fucking dare you," I scream.

She grabs my hair and I'm grateful it's not hard, just like my slap wasn't. "Shit," hisses Reggie before he pulls us apart. "I don't have time for this drama today. I have a biker to bring down." He takes my hand and pulls me inside. Malia is with her nanny and I smile to reassure her that I'm okay.

In the office, there are two large men. I eye them cautiously. Reggie puts his mobile on a stand on his desk and it rings.

Riggs' face fills the screen when he answers the video call. "Reggie, I hear you're out of luck," he says casually. "First the club, then the warehouse. Who knows what will happen next. Maybe your shipment that's due today will come under attack."

Reggie laughs, but it's low and menacing. "Nothing will happen to that shipment, Riggs. Not unless you want to watch Anna suffer," he growls.

"What?" I ask quietly, trying to keep the panic from my voice. The two men move towards me, each gripping an arm.

I struggle, but they're so much bigger and taller that I don't stand a chance. They move me into view of the camera.

"You can pretend that you feel nothing." Reggie smiles. "But I'm about to test that theory." He punches me hard in the stomach and I almost fall to the ground, but I'm hauled to stand straight again and one of the men rips my head back by my hair. Reggie stands behind me and holds a knife to my throat. "A slip of the hand could get very messy," he says grinning.

"Fuck you, Reggie," yells Riggs. I feel the blade nick the sensitive skin on my throat and I cry out. "You wouldn't hurt her!" Riggs shouts.

"Undress down to your underwear," whispers Reggie in my ear. I shake my head and a stray tear rolls down my cheek. He presses the blade harder and I hiss. "You know how much seeing blood turns me on." He holds the knife up for me to see the red-coated tip. "Now, undress."

I undress slowly. Eventually, Reggie gets pissed with me and orders the two men to remove my clothing. I stand before him in my underwear, knowing my body is covered in bruises, bite marks, and small cuts. Reggie moves the camera closer to give Riggs a better view. "You think I wouldn't hurt her when making her bleed is what I live for?" He smirks. "I will fuck her just for you and I'll cut deep enough to let her bleed out. You can have live footage as she takes her last breath."

"You piece of shit," yells Riggs angrily. "I'll slit your damn throat if you lay another fucking finger on her."

"And there you were saying you didn't have feelings for my wife." Reggie smiles again. The camera on Riggs' end goes wobbly and then Chains' face is there.

He smiles. "Hey, Anna, Reggie. Good to see you all. Sorry to cut it short, but we have some containers to unload at the docks. I trust that you have trucks waiting to take the loads?" he asks brightly.

"Finally, a man who talks sense," hisses Reggie.

"Sense is something I have a lot of. We'll be seeing you soon, Reggie." Chains winks and then the screen cuts out.

"Put her in the basement. If anything happens to those containers, your boyfriend will be very sorry," he warns me. "And so will you."

It's been hours. How long does it take to unload a shipment? I shiver. I'm still in my underwear and it's not exactly homely down here in the basement. The door opens and Crystal enters carrying a tray. "I got you some sandwiches. Reggie went out, but he's put extra security around this place." She also places a shirt and some shorts on the floor. "And I thought you might want some clothes, so . . . " I smile and get dressed quickly.

"Is Malia okay?" I ask. She nods her head. "There's a Mobile phone hidden under some clothes in Malia's wardrobe. The only number stored in it is for Riggs. Maybe he can come now and get us?"

"Without my evidence, there's no point. Besides, there's a full army of men upstairs. He'll be killed as soon as he steps foot near this building. And do you want to risk Malia being hurt?"

I shake my head sadly. "What if . . . " I sigh. "What if we let him hurt me? He told Riggs he'd hurt me if the shipment didn't get unloaded. He said he'd film it for Riggs. Would that be enough?"

"We're not putting you in danger. Besides, rape, battery, is it long enough to keep him inside? We want him for everything. He's doing so much bad shit that I don't want him to breathe the same air as me or anyone else in this city."

"What if I kill him?" I ask.

Crystal's eyes widen. "Are you fucking serious? You want to plan a murder with a cop?"

"You said it yourself, you don't want to breathe the same air as him. His world's falling around him, and we both know whatever he's arrested for, he'll be out in weeks. Nothing sticks to him. The only way to get rid of him is to kill him."

Crystal backs away. "You've lost your damn mind if you think I will have any part of that. Stop your talking and eat a sandwich. I'll find something on him that he can't wriggle out of."

"What if he does hurt me? Am I supposed to let it happen?" I ask. "Can't you at least get me something for protection?"

"You want me to give you a weapon now? Jesus, Anna. Listen to yourself." She slams the door closed and I hear the lock.

Half an hour later, Crystal returns. "I've come to collect your plate," she says. I look down at the untouched sandwich. "And Malia said you love cheese and crackers, so I got you a plate just in case you feel hungry later." I frown. I hate cheese. "Be careful though," she adds, laying the tray on the floor by my feet. "That cheese knife is really sharp."

I smile. The knife is at least six inches long and extremely sharp. "It's the only one I could find in the drawer," she says, picking up my old plate of food.

"Thanks. I'll save the cheese and crackers for later."

She nods her head and winks at me. "Also, check under the crackers," she adds before leaving.

Once the door is locked, I lift the crackers to find the small Mobile that Riggs gave me. I breathe a sigh of relief, turn it on, and call Riggs.

"Shit, Anna. I'm worried sick about you," he growls when he answers.

"Finn, do you ever regret meeting me?" I ask.

He chuckles. "Why'd ya ask me that?"

"All I've done is cause you grief. If I hadn't come into The Windsor that night, all of this could have been avoided."

"That's ridiculous. You coming to the bar that night with your sassy attitude was one of the best nights of my life. From the second you walked outta that place, I couldn't get my mind off you."

I smile to myself. "Same."

"Where are you now?"

"In the basement. Awaiting my punishment. I think he's lost his mind."

"You didn't tell me he was hurting you like that," he mumbles.

"What could you do? I thought coming back here would make it all stop. I thought he'd give you Ziggy and Michelle and you could go on with your life. I'm so naive when it comes to your worlds."

"You're innocent. There's nothing wrong with that. If I wanted a hard ass biker chick, then I'd take someone like Pinky," he says and I laugh.

"Pinky would kick your ass into shape," I say fondly. "Listen, if Reggie hurts me, if it all goes wrong, you have to help Eva get Malia for me. You can't let him raise her," I say seriously.

"Shit, Anna, it won't come to that. The police are tailing his trucks. They'll arrest him."

"No, they won't." I sigh. "Be realistic, Riggs. There's videos on his phone of girls being hurt and taking drugs, but Crystal said that's not enough. The blood-soaked towel isn't enough. Marshall being beaten isn't enough. They'll never get anything to stick to him that will keep him inside. He's gonna come home and hurt me. You have to prepare yourself and Eva for that." I take the knife and slip it in the waistband of my shorts.

"No!" he growls. "I'll call the mayor now and tell them he's got you in the basement. That's enough to get you out of there."

"And then what? I got a court order before and he broke it. He'll always come after me or Malia and I can't spend the rest of my life running. I just need you to promise me that you'll get Malia away from him." He doesn't reply. "Finn, please."

"Fine," he mutters. "I promise. But it won't come to that. Somehow, I'll get you out of there."

I hear Reggie's voice outside the basement door. "I have to go. He's back," I whisper.

"No, don't hang up. Hide the Mobile," he whispers. "I can track it."

I glance around in a panic and then stuff the mobile into my bra just in time as Reggie storms in. "Get up!" he yells, and I stand. "Your fucking boyfriend thinks I'm bluffing," he shouts, grabbing my arm roughly. He drags me out of the room and through the house. "And now I have the cops on my ass."

Outside, Crystal is holding Malia by Reggie's car. "Get her in," he growls.

"Where are we going?" I ask. Reggie opens the front passenger door and shoves me inside. Crystal fastens Malia into her car seat, then Reggie pulls Crystal towards him.

"Remember, when they come here, you tell them you know nothing. As far as you're aware, we're on a family day out." She nods her head and he kisses her roughly.

Reggie wheel spins out onto the road and speeds along. "Reggie, where are we going?" I repeat. "Slow down, Malia's in the car."

"Your boyfriend tipped off the cops. They stopped my trucks and they'll be looking for me soon."

"So you're on the run?"

"We're gonna lay low for a while." He moves in and out of traffic and I grip my seat. "I have someone on the way to bomb your little boyfriend's den," he adds and glances at me with a smirk. "One hour and he'll be dust."

"There're kids there, and women. They're all innocent in this."

"Nobody's innocent, Anna. They live there knowing that crime pays for their lifestyle and they make that choice to stay. You see me as the bad guy, but what he's doing is the exact same, only he has the mayor backing him. He isn't a nice guy just because he smiles and looks after his kid all by himself," he says bitterly. "He sells drugs that get kids hooked. He's responsible for the deaths of addicts too."

"Please slow down," I whisper.

"And he wants everything. Do you think he'll be the same nice guy when he controls the streets on my side too? It's a big job, Anna. He'll have whores at his fingertips. He'll soon forget about you."

"Why are you running from the police? You always get out of things. There's no way you'll go to prison," I say.

"Because, Anna, I have enough drugs in the boot of the car, to make London look like a snowy Christmas scene . . . and a dead body."

I whip my head to face him so fast that I hurt my neck. "A dead body?" I hiss. "Who the hell is in the boot?"

"It's a very long story, but let's just say the mayor thinks his daughter has ran away with her boyfriend. Parental differences caused an argument."

"Oh my god, you have the Mayor of London's daughter in the fucking back of this car?" I almost scream. "Why?"

"It was a last-minute thing," he says through gritted teeth. "I wasn't thinking straight, and she ran out in front of my car."

"You ran her over?" I ask.

"Not exactly, but I saw an opportunity." He smacks the steering wheel a couple of times. "Fuck, fuck, fuck." He's unravelling. I've never seen Reggie in this state before.

Malia begins to cry, and I reach my hand behind the seat to stroke her leg. "You're scaring Malia," I hiss. "How did she end up dead?"

"She wouldn't stop screaming and kicking in the boot. Everyone was looking as I drove past, so I strangled her."

I bury my head in my hands. "Oh my god. What are you going to do with her now?"

"I've got somebody meeting me at the service station on the motorway." He checks his watch. "Five more minutes and she won't be my problem."

"Where's Stephan? I thought he was your right-hand man, but I haven't seen him around in a while," I ask.

His knuckles turn white as he grips the steering wheel tighter. "He left months ago. Took a shit tonne of money and ran. Said I was getting too crazy, even for him." He laughs maniacally.

I sit back in my seat and hope to god that Riggs heard all of that.

We drive around to the farthest point at the rest stop, away from the services building. There's one truck parked there with the curtains closed. Reggie gets out of the car and taps on the truck window. "If you can hear me, Riggs, then I hope to god you have the cops on their way to us. The truck is white. The registration plate looks private, it's CAL007."

I watch the truck driver get out of the truck and shake hands with Reggie. They go to the back of the car and I use the mirrors to watch them get the girl out. She only looks around eighteen and I cover my mouth to keep the sob in. I glance in the back and Malia is asleep. *Thank god.*

The truck driver throws her over his shoulder, her lifeless body hanging limply. Anyone looking would assume she was passed out. "Shit, Riggs. Where are the cops? He's putting her in the truck. They'll miss him if they don't hurry," I hiss, hoping he can still hear me. As if my prayers are answered, the sound of sirens fill the air and I sigh with relief.

Reggie marches towards me and pulls my door open. He grabs me by the hair and pulls me out of the car. Police cars stop a few metres away and officers get out with guns pointed at us. "Get in the truck and drive at them," Reggie tells the truck driver.

"Don't be stupid, they'll shoot us all," I hiss as he tugs my hair tighter.

"Stay where you are. Put your hands above your heads and drop to your knees," yells one of the cops.

"You come any closer and I'll kill her," yells Reggie, pulling a small handgun from his back pocket and holding it to my head.

The air is filled with men yelling. Cops are shouting over and over for Reggie to drop his weapon and he yells back threats to kill me.

"Reggie, it's over," I whisper. "Let me go."

"No. If I go, then you go with me!" he warns.

"And who will look after our daughter?" I ask pleadingly. "Let me raise her away from this." I carefully reach behind me for the knife. I grip the handle tightly and release it from my waistband. My heart beats rapidly knowing the police might shoot when they see the weapon.

"Hands where we can see them," yells one of the cops.

"I don't have a gun," I yell back. "Please don't shoot me." As I say the last words, I raise the knife quickly and aim it over my shoulder, praying I hit a part of Reggie so that he releases me and doesn't pull the trigger. Reggie's hand releases my hair and I drop forward and away from him. I crawl quickly towards the police, who encourage me to move faster. A cop grabs me under my arms and hauls me back through the throng of police. There's yelling and then a shot is fired. "My daughter," I cry. "My daughter is in the car!"

The cop holding me yells into his radio. "Cease fire! There's a child in the car! Cease fire immediately."

I'm shaking so hard that my whole body is shuddering. The police move out and I can make out Reggie lying on the ground. My eyes are fixed on his jerking body. His hands are gripping his neck and he's making a choking sound.

Another officer rushes towards me cradling Malia to his chest. He places her in my arms, and I hold her tightly to me. Her body is wracked with sobs and I dread to think what she may have seen through the car window.

Chapter 20

RIGGS

The room is silent, and I can feel everyone's eyes on me. The muffled sounds of Malia's and Anna's sobbing come through the Mobile phone and I bow my head to contain myself. "She's safe now, brother," says Cree. I nod because I'm too choked with emotion right now to use words.

"They're taking her to get checked at the hospital as a precaution," says Chains, pulling his Mobile away from his ear. "Shall I tell the officer we'll meet them there?" I nod again and he relays that information.

"Arrange for Frankie to send the mayor's wife some flowers with our condolences and a large bottle of bourbon for the mayor," I say.

The connection between mine and Anna's Mobile is cut off from her end. Eva is outside church when I open the door. She looks at me expectantly.

"She's okay. They're both okay," I confirm. She throws herself into my arms and sobs into my chest. I hear Cree growl from behind me and I hold her closer just to mess with him. "I'll take you to see her," I say. "You can ride on my bike."

"She'll ride on my fuckin' bike," growls Cree, and I hold my hands up and smile.

"Okay, VP. She can go on your bike."

My mum brings Ziggy over to me and I kiss his head. "Can you keep an eye on Michelle, mum? I need to go and see Anna."

She nods with a smile and Ziggy suddenly looks brighter. "Is Malia coming?" he asks.

I smile and nod my head. "Yeah, Zig. She's coming home." He smiles wide. It's the first smile I've seen from him since we got him back. "And we're all gonna go on holiday. Me, you, Anna, and Malia," I add. He reaches for me and pulls me in for a hug. I realise he's been feeling just as lost without Malia as I have without Anna.

When we get to the hospital, we're ushered into a private waiting area. It often happens in places like this. We arrive in kuttes with our patch on and big boots and they're afraid we'll scare the other visitors.

I pace back and forth until the door opens and Anna stands there in a hospital gown.

We stare at each other for a few seconds before I march towards her and pull her to me. She wraps her arms around my neck, and I bury my nose in her hair. The scent of her strawberry shampoo is missing, but she still smells like my Anna. My heart warms as I hold her, and it hits me just how badly I need her.

"Can I get a look in?" asks Eva, tugging on my arm. I smile and release Anna to her friend. "Anna, I missed you so much," she sobs.

"I'm okay," she insists, stroking Eva's hair from her face. "Malia's asleep. I think all the drama has exhausted her."

"And Reggie?" asks Eva.

Anna shrugs her shoulders and looks to me to see if I know anything. I shake my head. "I'm waiting on a call," I say.

"You guys can go. I'm gonna be here a few more hours. They've taken blood from me and Malia and we need to wait for the results. They also ran a pregnancy test," she mutters, glancing at me.

I smile stiffly. It's not like I didn't know they were having sex. I can hardly get mad when she was just trying to survive. "I'll stay," I say.

"Really, it's fine if you want to go—" she begins but stops talking when I take her hand.

"Darlin', I'm staying right here with you and Malia," I say firmly and she smiles.

Malia wakes and her eyes fall on me. I get up and approach her bed quickly, hoping she doesn't cry and wake Anna, who's sleeping soundly in the bed next to her. "Hey, you," I whisper.

"Riggs," she mutters, holding out her arms. I pick her up and she snuggles against me. "Where's Ziggy?"

"He's waiting at home for you. He's so excited," I whisper. She lays her head against my chest and I settle back into the chair, pulling a sheet around her. I feel my eyes grow heavy and Malia's light snores tell me she's drifted back off to sleep. This feels right. My two girls are safe and there isn't a place I'd rather be. All we need now is to get back to Ziggy.

I hear voices. I'm not sure how long I slept for, but Malia is still snoring on my chest. "The pregnancy test came back negative," says a male voice.

"Thank god." Anna sighs. "Thank you so much for everything."

"This is the cream you'll need to apply to those nasty bite marks. The police officer will come to your home address to take your statement, but we've forwarded the pictures of your injuries to help with the case."

"Thanks," mutters Anna. "So, we can go?"

"Yeah. I just want to check we have the right address before you go," he says.

"Erm, that's not the right one. That's my old home address," says Anna, and then she reels off the clubhouse address. The doctor leaves and I smile. "What are you smiling at?" whispers Anna. I open one eye and she's looking down at me.

"You're coming home with me?"

"Well, someone's gotta take care of your ass." She sighs. "God knows what kind of bother you'll get in without me there."

I laugh and the movement wakes Malia, who rubs her eyes sleepily. "You girls will be the death of me," I say. "But I'll die a happy man."

Chapter 21

RIGGS

One Month Later

I kiss Michelle lightly on the head and wrap her into a tight hug. "Take care of yourself. Work at getting your life back on track," I say, and she nods against my chest.

"Thank you for everything, Riggs. I know I've been difficult, and you didn't have to put up with that. I'm grateful," she says. I nod in acknowledgment. "And I'll write to Ziggy every week."

"Yeah, that'll be nice," I say.

"Tell him I love him," she whispers, and her eyes fill with tears.

"Get well again and you can tell him yourself. This isn't forever, Michelle. Get sorted and we'll take it from there."

The Kings Reapers charter in Scotland will keep an eye on her for me, but she's staying with a good friend of my dad's. She's got a farm there and a shop where Michelle can work. A fresh start and new friends are what she needs to get her life on track. This is her final chance. Any slips after this will be the end of the road for us and I've made that clear. Now the drugs are out of her system and she's thinking clearly, maybe she's ready to make the changes.

I watch the taxicab drive away. Anna appears by my side and slips an arm around my waist. "I love you," she whispers.

"I love you too." I kiss her on her head and inhale the strawberry scent of her shampoo. "I want you in the shower in ten seconds. I'll give you a five-second head start," I say, and she eyeballs me.

"Don't start this again," she grins, shuffling away from me.

"Five," I begin to count, and she giggles.

"Riggs." She laughs. "Stop."

"Four . . ." She takes off and I leave it two seconds before I run after her.

Anna screams as she dodges in and out of the brothers who stare at our very public display of chase. I knock one or two as I try and squeeze my huge body through. "Sorry," I shout back at them. I catch her before she gets to the stairs and wrap my arms around her waist. "Not so fast, trouble," I whisper, and she shudders in my arms. "You know how hard I am for you right now?" I ask, pushing my erection into her back. "But I have some shit to say first."

I walk her back to the main room where I've gathered all of the Kings members and their families. I keep Anna in front of me to hide my bulging anatomy. "What's going on?" she whispers.

"Brothers," I say, and the room quietens down. "I think it's obvious why you're here. Some of you have been expecting this day since—"

"Since Anna swayed her cute ass into The Windsor that first time," shouts Chains, and the brothers laugh and cheer.

"I did not sway," she huffs. "I was annoyed."

"I'm taking her swaying ass and making her my ol' lady," I announce, and the cheers get louder. Anna turns in my arms and smiles up at me. "If you'll let me," I add quietly so that only she can hear.

"I'm glad you know who the real boss is," she quips.

"Always." I smile.

"Do I have to get a tattoo?" she asks. I nod my head. It's tradition for her to have my name somewhere on her gorgeous body. "Can I choose where?"

"You are the boss," I say, and she grins.

"Fine. I'll be your ol' lady, but only because I love your mum and your kid. I guess you're alright too."

I kiss her hard and she smiles against my lips. "Shower, now." I swat her ass and she takes me by the hand and leads me upstairs.

ANNA

It's been two weeks since Riggs laid claim to me, but it feels so much longer because we have been consumed with Reggie's trial. It was rushed through the courts because of the mayor. He wanted it put to bed to help his wife grieve and move forward. I'm not sure the loss of a child can ever be something you move forward from, but having met the mayor, he's not the emotional type.

I've spent the last three hours staring out this window as rain drizzles down the window of the courthouse café. Riggs places my third coffee down in front of me. The jury went out to reach their verdict at lunchtime yesterday, and here we are again today, still waiting.

I run over everything that I said in my head for the hundredth time. Reggie's defence lawyer was an ass and tried to completely rip my story apart, but luckily, Riggs recorded the entire car ride of conversation, right up until I cancelled the call. Hearing Reggie's confession to killing the mayor's daughter brought back memories of seeing her lifeless body.

It also came out in court that the truck driver had a history of necrophilia and he'd paid Reggie for her dead body.

I sigh and Riggs takes my hand. "I hate this waiting," I say.

"I know. We can leave if you like. I can ask the clerk to call us with the verdict," says Riggs. I shake my head. I want to look Reggie in the face when I hear his verdict because I'm certain he will be found guilty.

Crystal, whose real name is Rebecca, walks towards us. "They're going back in," she says with a smile.

The courtroom is big. It's a daunting experience and one I hope I never go through again. We file in one by one and fill the seats of the gallery. Most of the Kings Reapers are here for support and I love that I'm a part of their family. Eva holds my one hand while Riggs holds the other. I notice Cree's little finger resting against Eva's little finger on her other hand and I smile. He's so ridiculously shy that it's sweet.

"All stand," says the clerk as the judge enters.

"Be seated," mutters the judge. He reminds me of a tired looking headteacher. "Let's get straight to it, shall we," he continues, looking down at some papers the clerk hands him. "Can the foreman for the jury please stand?" A thin man stands and glances around nervously. This jury was selected from the outer parts of London, where they hoped Reggie would have no reach. The mayor wasn't letting him get off this time.

The judge continues. "For the first charge in the battery and assault of Mrs. Anna Miller, how do you find the defendant? Guilty or not guilty?"

The man coughs and the judge rolls his eyes impatiently. "Guilty," he says, and Riggs squeezes my hand. My eyes fall to Reggie and he's staring right back at me from his little glass-covered box. I smile triumphantly.

"For the charge in the murder of Elise Alice Knowles, how do you find the defendant? Guilty or not guilty?"

"Guilty, your Honour," says the man with a look of relief passing over his face.

I let out the long breath I didn't know I'd been holding. Reggie keeps his eyes fixed to mine. The wound where I stabbed his neck is visible and he now walks with a limp from the police officer shooting him in his leg.

"You'll never see Malia again," I say, leaning over the balcony so he can hear me amongst the chatter of the courtroom. "I'm filing for divorce, I'm removing your name from her birth certificate, and in time, she'll forget you ever existed," I say.

"You can't do that," he growls, and I smile wider.

"I have friends in high places, Reggie. It's already happening."

I sit back in my seat and turn to Riggs, kissing him. "It's over now." He smiles. "We can move on."

The judge rambles on about how sentencing will take place in another week, but he warns Reggie that he's facing a long time behind bars and that he's looking to impose the maximum sentence of life in prison with no chance of parole.

I leave the courthouse smiling from ear to ear. He'll never darken my doorstep again. Malia and I are finally free.

Riggs stops and spins me to face him, planting a big kiss on my lips. "Let's get the kids and go to Vegas." He smiles. "I want to marry you."

I laugh. "I have to wait for my divorce to be finalised," I say.

"No, you don't. I was waiting until this was over to tell you that it's all gone through. The mayor sanctioned it as urgent and, well, he pulled the right strings to make it happen on the promise that we invite him to the wedding reception when we return from Vegas."

I stare open-mouthed. "Oh my," I gasp. "I thought today couldn't get any better and then you go and tell me this."

"You know the guys are calling you Riggs' ruin, right?" he asks, and I laugh. "Because you've ruined me for every other woman out there. There's no one who comes close to you, Anna. Marry me?" He drops to one knee and I laugh nervously. People around us stop and watch as he pulls out a small box. "I'm the president. I don't do romance, but this seemed right, and Eva said you'd love this," he continues, glancing at her. She gives a small wave and smiles, the romantic in her finally getting to witness a grand gesture. "So?" he pushes, holding the box closer. A huge white gold diamond ring sits pretty, twinkling in the bright sunshine.

I nod my head and place my hands over my blushing cheeks. "Yes," I say. "I'll marry you." The gathering crowd around us clap and cheer as Riggs sweeps me up into his arms and spins me around.

"Good, because our flight leaves tonight," he whispers, and I laugh.

"I love you, Finn." I smile, and he kisses me, soft and gentle, cupping my face in his hands.

Eventually, he pulls back. "I love you too, Anna."

The End

A note from me to you

If you enjoyed Riggs' Ruin, please share the love. Tell everyone by leaving a review or rating on Amazon, Goodreads, or wherever else you find it. You can also follow me on social media. I'm literally everywhere, but here's my linktr.ee to make it easier.

https://linktr.ee/NicolaJaneUK

I'm a UK author, based in Nottinghamshire. I live with my husband of many years, our two teenage boys and our four little dogs. I write MC and Mafia romance with plenty of drama and chaos. I also love to read similar books. My favourite author is Tillie Cole. Before I became a full-time author, I was a teaching assistant working in a primary school.

If you'd like to follow my writing journey, join my readers group on Facebook, the link is above.

Printed in Great Britain
by Amazon